More Praise for Paula Fox

Desperate Characters

"Brilliant. . . . Fox is one of the
our way in a long, long time."

"A towering landmark of postwar realism. . . . A sustained
work of prose so lucid and fine that it seems less written than
carved."   —David Foster Wallace

The Widow's Children

"Chekhovian. . . . Every line of Fox's story, every gesture of
her characters, is alive and surprising."
                    —Christopher Lehmann-Haupt, *New York Times*

"Paula Fox is so good a novelist that one wants to go out in the
street to hustle up a big audience for her."
                              —Peter S. Prescott, *Newsweek*

Books by Paula Fox

Novels

Poor George
Desperate Characters
The Western Coast
The Widow's Children
A Servant's Tale
The God of Nightmares

Books for children

How Many Miles to Babylon?
The Stone-Faced Boy
Portrait of Ivan
Blowfish Live in the Sea
The Slave Dancer
A Place Apart
One-eyed Cat
The Moonlight Man
Lily and the Lost Boy
The Village by the Sea
Monkey Island
Amzat and his Brothers
The Little Swineherd and Other Tales
Western Wind
The Eagle Kite
Radiance Descending

Poor George

Poor George

Paula Fox

Introduction by Jonathan Lethem

W. W. Norton & Company
New York · London

Copyright © 1967 by Paula Fox
Introduction copyright © 2000 by Jonathan Lethem

First published as a Norton paperback 2001

Library of Congress Cataloging-in-Publication Data

Fox, Paula.
    Poor George / Paula Fox.
        p. cm.
    ISBN 0-393-32131-2 (pbk.)
    1. Manhattan (New York, N.Y.)—Fiction. 2. Juvenile
delinquents—Fiction. 3. Tutors and tutoring—Fiction.
4. Married people—Fiction. 5. Suburban life—Fiction.
6. Teenage boys—Fiction. 7. Teachers—Fiction. I. Title.
PS3556.O94 P66 2001
813'.54—dc21   00-048116
                                                      CIP

W. W. Norton & Company, Inc.
500 Fifth Avenue, New York, N.Y. 10110
www.wwnorton.com

W. W. Norton & Company Ltd.
10 Coptic Street, London WC1A 1PU

1 2 3 4 5 6 7 8 9 0

For Martin

Homely Doom Vibe

Introduction by Jonathan Lethem

"Who listens?"

An irresistibly compact and annoying question, posed by George, the title character of the book you hold in your hands. That question is like a pinprick of light in a dark surface: the only entrance you'll be offered. Better crawl through and see what's there.

First, an introduction that shouldn't be necessary. How good does an author or a book have to be to be reintroduced? To be pulled back into print by the devotional efforts of editors and writers (all of us only readers, really, when it comes down to it), pulled back against the unceasing tide of new titles, how good? I'm here to tell you how very, very good Paula Fox is.

It's hard to do more, though, when writing critically about an artifact as dense, distinctive, and self-contained as *Poor*

George, than be a gnat buzzing at the outer surface of a lozenge. The lozenge unmistakably needs to be swallowed and absorbed, which the gnat can't do. If it is swallowed and absorbed, though—as I've just done three times in a short span of months—an essence seeps through the body, then lives on the surface like a new set of nerves.

What I mean to say, as I circle my desk, trying to decide what to tell you about *Poor George*, is that I'm wearing the book as a skin. This skin is particularly tender to social loathing and self-loathing, to morbid confession disguised as chitchat, and, above all, to postures of self-willed innocence in human relations. Paula Fox writes with an almost crushing accuracy about these things, here and elsewhere. And if this isn't always a skin I'm completely eager to wear, perhaps I'm closer to understanding how a writer as great as Fox can linger for so long at a proximity from the acclaim and readership she plainly deserves. There's no justice, but maybe a certain inevitability, that a master of elucidating what's denied everywhere under the surface of human moments— and of measuring the texture of that insistent, howling denial—should find her own work denied, kept at bay at the edge of vision.

So who's this George who wants to know who listens? He's a schoolteacher, a husband, a Samaritan—a nobody, if you'll forgive me. George might be trying and failing to father a child, and he might also have an Achilles' heel in the area of unexamined bisexual longing—likely there are a few longings, his own and those of his loved ones, at which he'd be well advised to take a closer look. But really, here's the key thing about poor George: don't tell the guy, but *he's made of gorgeous sentences*. Sentences that are gorgeous because of how closely they listen. A vibrant, writerly intelligence shines everywhere through the bars of George's prison—in fact, the bars themselves might be said to be made up of the compressed and blinding sunlight of literary sensibility. Try for instance:

> He had to convince Ernest of—of what? Convince him that much had gone before, that he had not sprung from sticks and stones to find himself on a dead planet thinly covered with sidewalks leading nowhere.

Or:

> When she is silent she is very silent, George thought, and found himself interested in her. She vomits speech, then retreats, like some mud dweller.

Or:

> In that empty landscape where only the two trees and the toppling uprights of the shed gave shelter, they had stumbled towards each other, falling into the prickly dust in a thick, graceless embrace, their faces straining against each other's shoulders like two swimmers racing desperately for opposite shores.

The question is, *who listens to sentences like these?* Not George. George only teeters at knowingness, then retreats. Not only is he not as smart as the sentences that form him and the bars of his prison but, disconcertingly, crucially, he's not as smart as the sentences he's given to speak. Fox grants him the acid wit accorded the rest of her characters, but his tongue knows more than he does, as he completes his numbed and persevering daily route through himself and his life. George watches his wife cry:

> One large, luminous tear was on her cheek; dazzled by its brilliance, he watched it run under her chin and disappear. Perhaps, he thought, he was crazy, The weight . . . the weight of everything was stupefying.

I'd venture that the weight George staggers under is the weight of how much everything is forced to mean when you've tried to deny the meaning of what actually is.

Now the buzzing gnat part of me reminds me to inform you that *Poor George* is funny. Not "also funny" but essentially, vitally funny, in the perverse vein of Kafka and Flannery O'Connor. There are Diane Arbus photographs in prose here, as Fox offers her vision of bodies as poorly operated puppets:

> Four young men walked by. They were disparate in physical type but each face bore the same sullen inward look. They were thin, shaggy, book-carrying, slovenly, and their arms and legs appeared to have been glued on with little consideration for symmetry. "I have seen the future and it walks," George said. At that moment one of them turned and stared at Lila, at her prominent breasts. There was no expression on his face at all.

Here's another:

> The woman, red-haired and massive, was shaking a small boy whose head was encased

in a transparent bubblelike helmet. On it was
printed "Space Scout." From inside, the boy
gazed out coolly like a fish. A blind Negro,
his white cane poking out in front of him, hesitated and stopped. The woman shot a furious
glance in his direction, then banged on the
helmet with her knuckles.

Another gnat instinct I won't resist is to compare *Poor
George* to Fox's other masterpiece, *Desperate Characters*, if only
to draw in those familiar with the book that deservedly kicked
off the revival you're taking part in, lovely, faithful reader, by
picking up this one. *Poor George* was Fox's first published
novel, *Desperate Characters* her second. I felt echoes: Ernest in
Poor George is a kind of conflation of *Desperate Characters*' biting stray cat and its unglimpsed pillagers who desecrate the
country house, while Walling in *Poor George* mimics Charlie
Russel in *Characters* as a hipster-irritant-seer to contrast the
uptight male lead. What *Poor George* does that *Desperate
Characters* refrains from doing is explode. It feels like Fox tried
it once each way in her first two novels: tightening the screws
in *Characters* and letting the wheels fall off in *Poor George*. The
result is that *Poor George* is somehow both more disorienting
and more relieving—in the strict sense of tension released.

To my eye, that messy and funny explosion into overt drama
in its last sixty pages gently aligns *Poor George* with more or
less contemporary novels by Thomas Berger, Charles Webb, L.
J. Davis, and Bruce Jay Friedman. And, by reminding me of all
of them at once, it made me understand for the first time how
sixties literary critics might have been excused reaching for a
label to describe a certain flavor in American fiction of the
time—though the one they found, "Black Humor," was as inad-

equate as any label any writer was ever compelled to reject. I'm not even sure why I bring it up, except that *Poor George* is of its time, richly so. And that I miss a certain homely-doom vibe, which seemingly used to be more casually deployable, as in those novelists I've listed, and in films like Robert Altman's *Three Women* and Alan Rudolph's *Choose Me*, and in Randy Newman's songs from the same period.

Who reads? I'd never heard of Paula Fox, except as an author of children's books, before an editor pushed *Desperate Characters* at me three years ago. Three years later she's a favorite, and an influence on my own work. Since you might be grappling for context now the way I was then, I'd be ungenerous not to repeat some of what Jonathan Franzen and Andrea Barrett establish in their elegant introductions to *Desperate Characters* and *The Widow's Children* (Fox's fourth novel, republished in 1999): these books were critically acclaimed in their time, really. Compared by critics then and now to Chekhov and Melville and Muriel Spark and Nathanael West and Batman and Robin, really, and rightly. She's good, she's good, she's more than good. If it's amazing what can be recognized and forgotten (or denied), it's also amazing what can be restored, and Paula Fox is, I think, becoming the most encouraging revival from completely-out-of-print status since Dawn Powell. (Buzz, gnat, buzz.) What I mean to say is, for yourself, not for me or Paula or George, read the book. *Listen* to it.

Poor George

Chapter One

WHO LISTENS?

No one, said George Mecklin to himself. He had placed his chair so that he could see past the other teachers to a window where for a moment passers-by were framed as they walked down Ninety-eighth Street. The meeting had started at three. Now it was after four. Someone clicked the retractor of a ball-point pen. Someone lit a cigarette. Someone coughed. They had finished with the matter of the fall conference. The headmaster, Harrison Ballot, bent his head over his notes. His short arms and plump hands lay extended and motionless on either side of the papers on the table in front of him.

Above the dark brownstones which lined the street across from the school, George could see a strip of sky the color of tallow. The buildings appeared to be suspended in a viscous gray medium. Was it raining?

"If it was only the high school," began Ballot, looking up over the heads of his faculty, "but it's in the lower school too. The fifth grade is absolutely riddled with it."

"With what?" asked Harvey Walling, a math teacher.

Ballot's naked skull wrinkled as though something inside it had moved restlessly. "What? What do you think? Injudicious borrowing, that's what!"

"Cheating," said a short-haired woman from the English department.

"There are gradations," Ballot said softly.

"Gobble, gobble, gobble," mouthed the woman. She looked chagrined.

George stared at the window. Two men, dark, withered and thin-necked, bearing their heads like effigies on sticks, passed by quickly. Puerto Ricans? Then a huge Judy flashed into view, disappeared for an instant and bobbed back as if a lurking Punch had whacked her.

Muttering that the room had grown stuffy, George got up and went to the window and opened it a crack. The woman, red-haired and massive, was shaking a small boy whose head was encased in a transparent bubblelike helmet. On it was printed "Space Scout." From inside, the boy gazed out coolly like a fish. A blind Negro, his white cane poking out in front of him, hesitated and stopped. The woman shot a furious glance in his direction, then banged on the helmet with her knuckles. The blind man took a step forward and his foot landed on a garbage-can cover. Disconcerted, he stopped and appeared to reflect. At that moment the child wrenched off his helmet and tossed it into the street. The woman smacked his thin bluish cheek and raced after the helmet while the boy cried into one hand, the other gripped against his side. The Negro

4

thrust forward once more. A few raindrops streaked the window, as though the element which held the city so still had begun to melt. George returned to his chair.

"It must be stopped," Ballot was saying.

"But how? How indeed!" cried Lawrence Rubin, who taught history to the upper forms. He slapped the table top. No one liked him and no one answered him. Walling, sitting across from George, pulled the ends of his black mustache. He was wearing a red suède vest. George wondered if it was to attract women. He had heard that Walling painted.

Half asleep, George listened to the sounds of a committee being formed—there would have to be a special assembly; student council members must be consulted and advised; Ballot would write an editorial for the school paper. Rubin slumped in his chair. "The whole country's corrupt," he said to the ceiling. Walling was openly correcting math papers on the table. George ordered himself to listen. He looked down to see what tie he had on.

There was more—an argument over the choice of the senior play; a report on the apple machines in the recreation room (they were wrecked); a description of the newly installed language laboratory aspirated by the head of the language division. Time crawled up one side of the classroom clock and down the other. Then it was over.

With his coat half on, George made for the door. Ballot stood there bowing like a deacon, a faint smile on his white old cat's face, as the teachers filed out. He touched George's arm with one fat finger.

"How's the country?"

"Fine," George answered.

Rubin thrust himself between them, his large mouth

twitching in advance of his words, and George ducked out into the corridor.

He walked down Columbus Avenue to Eighty-ninth Street where his sister, Lila, had two rooms on the second floor of an old town house. Behind the large apartments fronting on Central Park West, the street breathed an air of decay and desolation. It had begun to rain hard; rain fell on the blackening façades of brownstones, on the open refuse cans where cinders turned a fleshy pink, on the toneless gray of the street where animal excreta slowly liquefied and refuse sidled sluggishly toward the drains.

On either side of the entrance to Lila's building two cement planters held a harvest of rusty nails sunk into the cement at two-inch intervals. As George rang the downstairs bell, a swollen gray cat sitting on the edge of a planter reached out a paw and jabbed at a nail. Aware of only a great emptiness in which he and the cat stared incuriously at each other, he jumped at the answering ring.

Lila Gillis opened the door of her apartment wearing a cowl-like object over her hair. As she peered out into the dark hall, the cowl slid to her shoulders.

"You! What a surprise! Come in. I suppose you've only got five minutes? Claude, push off!" She tried to shake free from her seven-year-old son, who clutched her around her waist. As quickly as she disentangled his fingers from her belt, he grabbed handfuls of her skirt. Claude's head was covered with a paper bag. He made no sound as he struggled to hold onto her.

"I've got more than five minutes," George said as he stepped into the room.

"We've just come from the store." She wrenched loose from the boy.

"Claude, Claude . . ." called George. The boy shook his hooded head. "Would you like a plastic space helmet?"

"You'd better get one for me," said Lila. "As usual, everything is hanging by a thread."

George turned on the gooseneck lamp which gripped a bookshelf with its rusty claw. The light shone on the marble front of a blocked-up fireplace. A child's red truck was garaged in the shallow hearth. The rest of the room was in shadow, and there was a smell of dust, as though the windows had been closed for a long time.

"My job ends in a week. They told me this morning," Lila said. He turned to her. "Don't get scared," she said, and smiled then. "I didn't get fired. The job simply ran down."

"You're well out of it."

"You're always saying that to me about something or other, aren't you?"

"You need a real job."

"Do you want a cup of tea? Awful damned room, isn't it?"

"You're always holing up in some half-baked rescue league."

"Half-baked? Mental health is everybody's darling. I wrote fine letters to the crazy rich for money for the crazy poor. Campaigns end. Generals go back to their dusty rooms."

"You ought to remarry."

"I'll make some tea."

Claude was holding out his arms and shaking his wrists up and down. His hands flopped at the end of his arms like cotton-filled gloves.

"Quit that!" Lila said sharply. The boy ran off into the

bedroom. George felt Lila watching him. Did she know he found Claude repugnant?

"What about part-time teaching? You always liked making things. You could teach art."

She made a wry face. "Pipe cleaners and paste?"

He must have uttered a sound of disapproval because she held out her arms suddenly, palms up, asking to be understood. He remembered how when they were children, after Lila had hit him, she would stand back and extend her hands toward him in the same way. He sat down.

She let her arms fall and stood looking down at him. "I'm getting old," she said. "I think about the past all the time now. Every morning I wake up with one of Mama's homilies on my mind. She was always talking about preserving things. Do you remember how she covered everything? The whole house was a tea cozy. But everything does wear out, doesn't it? She must've thought about death a good deal. Do you think she did?"

"I don't know what she thought about. Do you need money?"

She was silent.

"I can give you a check for fifty dollars right now."

Claude came back. He had taken off the paper bag. On his small fair face there was a look of concentrated distaste as though what he saw, now that he could see, was unalterably offensive to him.

"I can manage," Lila said. "You need your pennies."

"Come here and talk to me, Claude," George said.

Claude flung his arms around his mother. "Juice!" he cried.

"Then let me go." Holding on, Claude pushed her to the pullman kitchen.

"You're not letting your mother walk," George said.

"Give it up," Lila said.

As she bent over to hand the boy the glass, the large knot of brown hair at the nape of Lila's neck loosened. Her skin was clear and pale, and where George's features were somewhat stubby, her's were fine and thin. Yet she looked plain to him. She filled a small pan with water and placed it on a burner. He suddenly thought her very tiring. There was a rip in her skirt, and she slumped over the stove in an elderly fashion.

"What about teaching? I can ask around."

"All right," she said without looking at him. "If you want to."

"For God's sake!"

The boy began to run wildly around the room, shouting *"Alors!"* Lila turned and watched him dispassionately.

"They teach them French in that Episcopalian hothouse he goes to. Or so they say," she said.

Claude picked up the red truck and brandished it.

"Alors, yourself," Lila said.

While they were drinking their tea, Lila asked George how he found the country. It was clear she was uninterested.

"Isn't Emma lonely by herself all day?"

"She hated the city."

"She could still be lonely."

"She comes into town."

"Oh, those country Sundays. How I detested them when we lived in Huntington. Sometimes people came to see us, and when they got ready to leave, I used to want to beg them to take me with them."

"It's only been a month," George said. "We haven't had

9

a chance to be disappointed yet." Thinking of his wife, he fell silent. He imagined she was sitting down in some room in the house. Seated, Emma seemed far away. Silently he ordered her to get up. It seemed strange to him that he could not visualize her walking. Claude spun the wheels of his truck.

"Are you making a plan for me?" Lila asked. She smiled at him as though she pitied his poor plans.

"Come up next weekend," said George. "We'll figure out something." He stood up and took ten dollars from his wallet. "Take it," he said.

"Don't you want something else? A piece of cheese?"

"I have to catch the train."

She held out her hand, and he placed the bill in it. At the door he paused. Except for the circle of light from the lamp he had turned on, the room was dark. Claude thrust the truck at him. Lila had one foot out of her shoe. What would they do when the door closed? He touched her arm, wishing he could help her.

"Don't you ever think of Mama?" she asked sadly.

"Sometimes," he replied.

"I remember everything that ever happened to me until I was ten," she said. "But not much after that."

He didn't know what to say.

The train smelled of damp pipes. It moved sluggishly through a wan landscape over which the darkening sky seemed to pulsate faintly. George, thinking of his mother, wondered how Lila's memory of her could be so different from his own. The winter that George was eight and Lila thirteen, Mr. Mecklin had died of a heart attack. He had been shoveling a path through the snow from the house to the street. George and his mother were watching the shovel-fuls of snow fly up and fan down when suddenly Mr. Meck-lin had leaned on the shovel as though to rest. Then he had pitched forward abruptly.

His mother had been holding a crochet needle in her hand. Had she plunged it into her other hand at the moment his father had fallen? Had his mother really stopped speaking to him from the time they had stood at the window together until she was old and ill? A body fallen like a tree, a self-inflicted wound, a silent house, the friends in school who had stared at him for a week or two as though they'd never seen his like before . . . Had it really been like that? Lila couldn't tell him. She was no help, for whatever point she might start from she always ended up with herself.

During the last years of Mrs. Mecklin's life, she had developed cataracts in both eyes. Behind her special glasses her glance was magnified, and it had seemed full of disdain and bitterness. His last gift to her had been a special deck of cards whose enlarged symbols made it possible for her to play solitaire. She had cheated openly. When Lila came to visit, she had often let the deck slip from her lap and watched with an ironic smile as Lila scrambled about the floor gathering the cards together.

Then one evening Lila had come home to show off a diamond engagement ring. She was living in New York City by herself, and she disliked the long subway ride, then the trolley out to Warburton Avenue in Yonkers. She was flustered and irritable, and she thrust the ring under her mother's nose. Rather bitterly, she had described how she had covered her hand in the subway to avoid arousing someone's cupidity. Mrs. Mecklin had said, "If you're so

11

afraid it will be stolen, why don't you swallow it?" George had stood up and for a second had seen a flash of fear in Mrs. Mecklin's sick old eyes. "A glass of water, please, George," she had asked humbly. He had pitied her, then.

Lila's diamond ring had turned out to be the sum of her good fortune. Having given it to her and having married her, her husband, Philip, had settled into a melancholy absorption with making his life earthquake-proof. As the New York agent for a Vermont insurance company, he saw the hazards of almost everything.

George had always wanted to help Lila. But he had never been able to do much except unlatch the door after midnight when she, then in her late adolescence, had begun coming home in the early hours of the morning, hectic and disheveled, the hand which gripped George's cold and damp, as he led her upstairs in the dark and past their mother's bedroom.

With a prolonged shudder, the train pulled into the Harmon station. In the parking lot, George's secondhand English Ford sat under a layer of coal dust.

Driving home, he forgot about Lila. Everything he looked at consoled him: the leafless trees, the rain-blackened rocks, a shabby frame house in whose dark depths he perceived the glow of a shadeless light, the stream which paralleled the road, a boy in a yellow slicker pushing a bicycle up a hill. In the middle of the reservoir, a man sat in a rowboat, huddled over a fishing rod. A black dog raced in front of the car and leaped into the water, then swam straight for the boat like a plumb line dropped into the gray lake. George stopped the car and let the motor idle. The dog's tail whipped the water. George could hear a wet scratching of claws as the dog tried to climb the gunwale.

12

Suddenly the fisherman brought his arm out and down, lifting the animal into the boat—there was a rattle of oar-locks, a scattered sound of the dog's nails as it shook itself. The man leaned forward and put his hat on the dog's head. George heard his laugh, a quick burst, and then the dog's answering bark.

The scene preoccupied him the mile or so he had still to drive. He envied the man his solitude. Could one cultivate a taste for it? He read a good deal, but usually when Emma was in the room. If she left, his attention wavered. He supposed his nature was essentially gregarious; even his dreams were filled with conversations and half-perceived faces.

He made a left turn where the reservoir road intersected Abraham's Lane, then drove up a rise passing the Palladino house, a large structure in the colonial style with green shutters fanning out from every window. A hundred yards behind it was the Mecklin cottage, and behind the cottage, scattered over a broad slope, an apple orchard. He drove into the double garage around which the little house was built.

He switched off the ignition and sat for a moment, his eyes fixed on the windshield, his breathing shallow. The stillness felt voluptuous; all the forces of his life were held in abeyance by the pale, empty moment. Then, as though the oncoming night were disgorging itself of an irritant, there was an explosion of wings, and George turned to look out the back window of the car, up toward the orchard. A flight of crows drew a black line across the sky.

As George stepped out into the garage, a breath of wind stirred the tattered newspapers lining the bushel baskets stacked in one corner; it fluttered the dust-laden spiders' webs hanging from the ladder by the window, and brought him the smell of spring. It was slight—a damp wind, a taste of damp earth. But standing alone in the garage, feeling the seasonal quickening in the air, he was assailed by an undefined but powerful sense of possibilities. It seemed a curious thing that, as a man vaguely oppressed as far back as he could remember, he should feel touched, if only lightly, by luck.

The back door was open.

"Emma?"

There was no answer. She might be sleeping. She might even have taken a walk. He turned off a dripping tap in the kitchen. As he walked into the living room he thought he heard the radio playing faintly upstairs and he called Emma again. When there was no response, he opened his briefcase and took from it a worn copy of *Moby-Dick*, along with a handful of blue notebooks in which were written the answers to an examination he had given his ninth-grade English class. Most of them would have written three pages on the symbolism of the whale's whiteness. Most of them would not have read the book at all. He didn't like it himself; the passion for revenge, he thought, was too alien to him. He placed book and examination papers on the card table he used for a desk. The whale wasn't white at all—it was pale with exhaustion from being hounded by a New England autocrat.

As he started up the stairs the back of his neck prickled delicately. His legs felt thick, heavy. What was wrong with him? He steadied himself against the banister and climbed up to the small upstairs hall. He was about to go into the bathroom when he caught sight of a slight movement of the

14

door to the unused bedroom. His heart began to pound. He felt faint, and when he heard his own breathing, he was struck with terror.

He wanted to run. But danger itself held him fast. "Move!" he groaned. Then with an explosive cry, he flung himself against the door, pushing it until the resistance of the body behind it would let him go no further. He kicked it savagely and heard himself pleading with whatever it was to come out . . . for God's sake . . . come out!

"You're breaking my head," a voice cried. George backed away. Someone snuffled. He waited. Then shaping and straightening his crushed hat, a boy of eighteen or nineteen slid sideways from behind the door. They stared at each other, then the boy pouted and pinched his hat.

"Look at that! I just had it two days."

"Don't move," George said.

"Who's moving? You know how much this hat cost me? It's wrecked!"

"Sit down!"

The boy sat on the mattress of the spare bed, still turning his hat with short, blunt fingers.

"Who are you?"

The boy placed his hat on the bed and looked at it.

"What's your name?"

"Ernest."

"Ernest what?"

He shrugged.

"What if I call the police?"

"Go ahead."

"Is it worth it? To take the chance?"

"Worth what?"

"The police."

Ernest smiled. "You always leave your house unlocked?"

"I could turn you in," George said. The trembling in his legs had stopped.

"I didn't take anything."

"Did you ever hear of breaking and entering?"

"I didn't *break* in. I just walked in."

George struck him on the shoulder. The boy rolled over on his back and drew up his legs. Stricken, George bent over him. Ernest looked up at him without expression. Then he lowered his legs slowly.

"Get out!" George cried. The boy righted himself and stood up.

"Out!"

"You say it and you say it again. I told you. . . . I didn't take anything. I never do. I like to see the inside when the people are out. That's all."

It was only then the thought of Emma, stuffed into a closet, dead, violated, moved dreadfully in his imagination like the fronds of a submerged plant. He ran to the door. Ernest was behind him. "She went out," he said. "Out to the orchard. Then I came in."

George pointed at the stairs. Ernest started down.

"I've been in all the houses near the reservoir," Ernest said quickly. "Like your neighbors right there . . . She's a lush. She drinks and he plays. That's the one thing I ever took. A note some girl wrote him. You want to know what it said? I know it by heart." He stopped and turned. "I'll say it to you," he offered.

"That's rotten."

"You know the Devlins? They've got gin in stone bottles . . . a thousand records. They owe money—more than you got."

George raised his hand. The boy ducked.

"I don't want to hear any more."

At the bottom of the stairs now, Ernest swiveled around the banister. He looked reflectively at the chipped wood.

"Did you turn the radio on?"

"Yes," Ernest said, and he laughed softly.

"Sit down," George said sternly. Ernest fell indolently into a chair.

"Why aren't you in school?"

"At this time of day?"

"You don't know what you're doing. Do you?"

"Do I what?" Ernest took a cigarette from a crushed pack on the table next to the chair. He saw George look at it. He held it stiffly for a minute, then George waved his hand. Ernest took a straight match from his pocket and lit it with his thumbnail.

"Where do you go to school?"

"I was held back in the last year. So I don't go."

"What are you? Nineteen?"

"Almost eighteen."

"What about the draft?"

The boy looked mildly interested. "Yeah?"

"The army."

"Which army?" he asked. He stood up. "You going to do anything?" He put on his hat. "Because I'm leaving."

"Do you live with your parents?"

"One puking drunk. You can tell him all about me. . . . He won't do anything much."

"Wait . . ."

"I'm too old to go to school. What are you looking at my hat for? Listen . . . I *want* to go now."

But George didn't want to let him go. He stood in front of Ernest blocking his way to the kitchen. He was experiencing something extraordinary; he felt a nervous exuberance which made it painful for him to stand still. "I'm a teacher," he said. Ernest looked at him impassively. "You'll get caught," George shouted.

"You caught me."

The power of his impulse impelled George forward. The boy drew back. "You must get through school," George said. He heard the intensity in his own voice. Afraid he would alarm the boy, he tried to speak without emphasis. "There's no place to go any more if you don't finish up. It's not the way it used to be. I can help you. I can show you short cuts. What was it that got you down? Listen, Ernest, education's the pass, the key. . . ."

Listening, but not to George, Ernest shook his head almost imperceptibly. His eyes were vague, but his narrow body expressed a kind of nervous readiness. His dark hair and eyes, the faint amber cast of his skin gave him an impermeable look. He was, George thought, almost beautiful. His features were purely linear, like those of wooden saints in cathedral niches. His narrow-lipped mouth was finely delineated, his cheeks long and flat. But when he turned, how different he was! Then his mouth was thin as thread; his lynxlike lid suggested secretiveness. He seemed bloodless.

Ernest walked past George to the kitchen entrance and instantly retreated, cupping his hand around his cigarette, which he thrust behind him. Emma had come in.

She stood in the doorway, looking from George to the boy.

"I wondered where you were," George said quickly. "Did you go for a walk?"

"Yes. A short walk," Emma said, staring at Ernest.

"Not much sun today?"

"It rained this morning."

"The meeting was longer than I expected. Then I stopped by to see Lila."

Ernest brought the cigarette to his lips, inhaled strongly and blew the smoke straight up. Was it a message? The moment stretched.

"This is Ernest, Emma," George said, finally. "He needs some help with schoolwork."

Emma looked bewildered; then she nodded and took off the jacket she was wearing, letting it drop on the couch. Ernest looked at it.

"It's wet," he said to no one in particular.

"It'll dry," Emma replied. She walked on to the staircase. The boy slipped into the kitchen and George followed. Emma might have been kinder. After all . . . a young boy. Sometimes he thought her coolness not so much a cover as the thing itself, an emptiness. There wasn't anything so puzzling about Ernest's presence that she even had to abandon good manners, was there?

Ernest stood at the kitchen door, his hand on the knob. "You'd better quit all this," George said in a low voice. Ernest laughed soundlessly. "It isn't remotely funny. Someone else might turn you in."

Ernest looked at him reflectively. "This is the first time I've been caught," he murmured.

"Didn't you hear me drive in?" George asked.

"It was too late. I thought I could jump through the window onto the roof over the porch. But the window was stuck." He shrugged. "I don't know." The knob turned in his hand. George saw how much he wanted to go. He felt angry and suddenly exhausted.

"How do I know you didn't take something?" he asked harshly. Ernest, his eyes on George's face, pulled out the lining of his pockets, one by one. A small pebble fell on the floor. Then he held out his hand, opening his fingers slowly. Two nickels lay in his palm.

"You'd better stay the hell out of peoples' houses," George said.

"How come you didn't tell her?" Ernest asked. George stooped to pick up the pebble. Something about the impersonal curiosity in Ernest's voice had made him flush. And he was ashamed he had forced the boy to empty his pockets. He stood there, the pebble in his hand.

"If you want help, if you're serious about finishing school, I'll see what I can do."

"If you want to . . ."

"If I want to! All right. I'll get in touch with you after I see about my schedule. What's your last name? Where do you live?"

"I'll come here. If you're out, I'll go."

"That won't work."

"I'm not going to make it," Ernest said indifferently. "Don't waste your time."

"How often can you come?"

Ernest didn't answer. He opened the door an inch and squinted one eye as he looked through the opening.

"Don't you want to try?"

"I'm going."

"My name is George Mecklin."

"Yeah . . . I know. . . ." He opened the door and stepped out into the garage.

As George watched him walk down the drive, from the living-room window, he realized there might have been a dozen things with his name on them Ernest could have found. He turned on a light, and the room grew pale, like a face drained of color. He was chilled and unsettled.

Emma moved about above. Then the sound of her footsteps stopped. She was looking down at him from the top of the stairs.

"Did you leave the radio on?" she asked. He looked at the pebble that was still in his hand; it was sticky, like a gumdrop.

"I guess I did," he answered. She continued to stare at him. She is considering what I said, George thought, because she knows I don't leave radios on. He dropped the pebble behind the radiator.

"I don't know what to wear tonight."

He hurried to suggest a dress. He wasn't up to a clothes list, itemized in a monotone to assure him she was being especially scrupulous not to reproach him for the state of her wardrobe.

"Not that one," she said. "It's shiny."

"We're only going to the movies," he said. She left him riffling through the pages of a blue book. "*Moby-Dick* is an American classic because—" He dropped the book, repelled by the fat, self-admiring letters and their plump, anatomical capitals. That would be Mary Lou Whimple, whose constant smile of infant irony made him especially careful when he marked her papers. He had begun to hate her. One had to be fair to people one hated. He let the book fall back to the table.

It had grown damply dark. A dim light shone from the Palladino house, a near ship in a fogbound sea. The living room felt tacky. George listened to the country silence. The incidents of the day grouped themselves in his consciousness like a charade waiting to be titled—the blind Negro, the swimming dog, Walling's red suède vest, Lila's sly smiles of defeat, that moment when he had felt lucky, and Ernest.

Deliberately he turned his attention to money, a subject guaranteed to knock out all other contenders. They would have a little more from now on even though Emma was only working three days a week at Columbia where she was a junior librarian. The ostensible reason for quitting full-time work was that she would be able, one of these days, to return to school to complete the requirements for senior librarian. Actually they had both been worried about her continual fatigue. Emma had said she would certainly have to rest up if they ever wanted to have a child. They had decided they would somehow *know* when they were ready for that.

The car would cost more now, what with extra fuel and upkeep, but there would be a saving on the insurance. On a yellow piece of paper which George kept in a breast pocket, transferring it to whichever of his three jackets he was wearing, he had assessed their new financial situation the morning after they had moved out from the city. In small numbers, in straight columns, the dollar signs written in green ink, he had covered every eventuality. It had given him deep satisfaction, that piece of paper. It was a claim for order. Yes, the paper covered every eventuality, he thought now, but the money didn't.

The furniture looked shipwrecked. They had planned to recover what was recoverable and heave out what was borrowed or inherited, but in the end they had loaded everything on the moving van. Emma had thrown a purple serape over the torn upholstery of the big chair. She had begun but not finished several pillows—the unseamed edges were lumpily stuffed into their own cases. She had borrowed an electric sander and taken the black finish off an end table but had given up on the round legs. Tacks and pins held their household together. In a corner stood a basket filled with scraps of material with which Emma planned to make a patchwork quilt. Two sections of an alto recorder—the third had disappeared during the move —lay on a Penguin booklet of Handel melodies, and a straw basket of the kind sold in Japanese shops was placed in the center of the table in front of the couch. The only object in it was an Aztec fetish, a particularly hideous one, George thought, Emma had picked up off the ground during a month's vacation in Zacatecas. She often paused by the table and absently rolled the figure about with an indifferent finger. It was, she said, her only authentic souvenir. He glared at the little figure with its malignant stone grin directed at the ceiling. He had hoped it would be lost during the move.

His hands in his pockets, his shoulders hunched over, George pressed his forehead against the window. Why was everything so shabby? Between them both, they ought to have enough money to live simply, cleanly. Emma said they lived as though the depression had not ended. But wasn't shabbiness a minor affliction? Was it really anything to *think* about?

Suddenly he pictured himself throwing out everything they possessed, sweeping out every corner of the little house, leaving only the washed, sweet air of the country in their four rooms. Then, frightened at the prospect of such nakedness—what would they be without their little wretched accretion of objects?—he ran upstairs.

Emma, bundled in her thick bathrobe, was lying in bed reading a paper Simenon. She glanced up briefly. George took a clean shirt from his bureau and removed the cardboard stiffener.

"Where did you find him?" she asked.

"He found me," replied George. At once his discovery of

Ernest, the fleshy feel of the door as he had pressed himself against it, came back to him, more vividly felt now than then.

"Where did he come from?"

"Peekskill, I suppose."

"He walked here?"

"It's only a mile or two."

"How did he know you were a teacher?"

"People know everything in the country."

"George, let's go to Mexico for a year."

"Sure."

"You mean it's out, then? Forever?"

"Someday we might."

"Please. Tell me about that boy."

"He dropped out of school. He was held back in his senior year."

"Was he just hanging around outside when you got home? I didn't see him before I went out."

He sat on the bed and felt for her feet beneath the robe. They lay in his hands, cold and narrow and still.

"Are you worried?"

She pulled her feet back and sat up straight. The book fell to the floor. "It was so eerie today," she said. "Everything so empty. I couldn't get much done. The house scared me. I don't know why. I don't know. . . . I saw a crow and thought it was fall . . . everything so gray." Her face was animated. He forgave her silently for her lack of grace with Ernest.

"Why didn't you drop in on the Palladinos?"

"They don't live there," she answered. "They haunt the place. She never comes outside, and he goes off in the morning with his clothes all wrinkled as though he'd slept in them. She sets the children out on the doorstep like milk bottles, then shuts the door. The kids are so peculiar. They sit there on the step with little things in their hands, toys of some kind I suppose, and pass them back and forth to each other until she comes to let them in again."

The day they had moved in, Mr. Palladino had walked slowly up the drive and asked with a certain deference if he could be of any help. He seemed uncomfortable; perhaps he had felt intrusive. George wondered at the bland smile, the curious air of uncertainty. He was dressed in a pale brown corduroy suit, and his shirt was faintly soiled. He had made an arrangement with George—continued, he said, from the former tenants—to use half the garage for his car, offering to pay a few dollars a month for the space. George had refused the money, and Palladino had nodded as though he had expected as much.

"He looked nice," George said.

Emma snorted. "Nice! An actor . . . A ladies' man."

"How do you know what he is?"

"Minnie Devlin told me," she said.

"Minnie Devlin sneers at rain. . . . She laughs people to death."

"She wasn't sneering. Anyhow, just look at his face. An actor's face, ripe and rotten."

He looked at her in surprise. "What's the matter with you?" he asked.

She laughed irritably. "I don't like pretty men."

Minnie had found the house for the Mecklins. Emma had known her briefly in Chicago. Just out of college, she had attached herself tenuously to an amateur theatrical group Minnie was organizing. Shortly after Emma left for New York, Minnie wrote that she had dropped the theater and taken up marriage again. A year later Emma had received a card announcing the birth of Trevor, ten pounds. "Shows you what peasant stock can bring up" Minnie had written on it somewhat prematurely. Last year she had turned up in New York. Chicago wasn't big enough for Charlie Devlin. The Mecklins hadn't met him yet. He was frequently out of town hunting down people for his radio program, "Happy People." Minnie said she was starting a talent agency. George found her tedious and vicious, but Emma said she was funny. When she had telephoned about the little house in the country, George had agreed, if reluctantly, that it was a good thing Emma had kept up with her. Next weekend they were finally going to meet Charlie. The Devlins were giving a party on Saturday.

Dutch gin and debts.

"What are you scowling at?"

George started guiltily. But if Mrs. Palladino was always home, how had Ernest gotten in, he was wondering? He got to his feet abruptly, pushed a chair back into a corner and pulled the shade down on the window which faced the Palladino house.

"You take her seriously," Emma said. "She's just a clown."

"What did you do all day?" he asked, thinking of Palladino, his domestic pocket picked by Ernest, his character anatomized by funny Minnie.

"I filed the spices. They were so dirty, the tops of the cans were still smeared with city grease."

"You filed them?"

"Alphabetically," she said. He laughed. She looked at him coldly. He supposed she had meant to illustrate the day's boredom. "I found this thing in the orchard," she said and, slipping her hand into the pocket of her robe, drew out a red water pistol, its muzzle broken. "I mean! That's some day! Isn't it?"

"It takes time. We've lived in the city too long. Wait till spring comes."

"While I was in the orchard," Emma continued, "an old man jumped up behind me."

Were they being invaded? George asked himself.

"He must have been watching me for a long time. When I turned around there he was, hanging on to a tree branch and grinning."

"Maybe we'd better get a dog."

"He was feeble," she said. "He muttered something. I nodded, and he disappeared. Maybe I imagined him!" She laughed excitedly, and he turned from the closet door to look at her. She looked much as she had when he had met her eight years ago, retaining her thin pale young girl's quality, her head outlined as with a charcoal pencil by a line of fine black hair which she wore in a loose tie in the back. Sometimes when she impatiently tied a string around her hair and wore a cotton skirt and sneakers, she reminded him of one of those wan girls who drift around the periphery of the bohemian world of any city, suffering so intensely yet silently from displacement that they seem heroic.

She was quite different when she dressed for work or an evening out: neat, self-contained, remote, sitting apart from him with her bony delicate ankles placed side by side on the floor.

"You're gaining weight," she said. He had been dressing slowly, thinking about her, relieved she had apparently forgotten about Ernest. Ernest who? He looked into the mirror Emma had nailed to the wall. It cut off his head unless he stooped. It was true—he had always been stocky, but now his belly protruded slightly. He didn't want to be one

27

of those fair fleshy men. He sighed heavily. Never as a young man had he imagined himself at thirty-four. In six years he would be forty. He buttoned his shirt hastily.

"How's Lila?"

"All right." There was no point in telling her that Lila had lost her job. Her face guarded, she would try to discover how much money George intended to give his sister.

"I asked her up next weekend. You don't mind, do you?"

"Why should I? If she could board Claude, I'd be more enthusiastic."

"He's not so bad."

"What do you mean! He's certifiable. Or else he does it on purpose. Either way . . ." She began to dress, and for a while they were silent, moving around each other familiarly.

Then they were dressed and facing each other at the bedroom door, he in his dark suit, she in her black dress. We still have time for everything, he thought.

The Palladino house was dark as they drove by it.

"All asleep," he said.

"All dead," Emma said.

They drove along Abraham's Lane toward the Peekskill turnpike. "I didn't like that boy," she said.

"You don't know him."

"Do you? I don't understand how he got there . . . or why."

"No, I don't know him. How can I judge him?"

"Huff, huff!" she blew out her cheeks. "Some of us are fair and some of us are rats!"

A gust of wind scattered leaves in front of the car's headlights. "Listen!" George said. In the wake of the wind he caught once again the odor of earth.

They stopped at a restaurant on the highway. It was

28

shaped like a windmill, and several cars were drawn up around it. As they walked toward the entrance they saw, in the yellow strip of light from a window, a child's doll, its lumpy arms upraised, its glass eyes shining, half buried in the gravel of the parking area. "Help!" squeaked Emma. "The Arabs have left me here to die!" George laughed, and something serious floated out of his mind; he kissed his wife's girlish neck.

Behind their cardboard menus their glances raced from entree to price. The waitress stood next to their table; her red arms bulged at the sleeve endings of her uniform, as though she were slowly growing out of it. The plastic mats, the hurricane lamp, the soiled pretentious menu, the wait-ress with her expression of patience in a hurry, and the humble, clotted ketchup dispenser were the elements of a set piece to which they returned again and again. How could he have told of their thousand evenings of the same entertainments without reference to these tangible mani-festations of tedium and habit?

Amid the impersonal debris of the outside world, Emma and George grew personal. Sleazy restaurants, bloated cars, the ravaged countryside bleeding into the new highways, the plug-ugliness of modern life gave their being together a moral character. On their evenings out they joined one another: commiserating about what didn't really matter to them.

Later, after the movie, they recalled the films they had liked as children. Then they left the main highway and turned off onto the blacktop road. George reached over and touched her, and in the dim light from the dashboard he saw his pink hand cupping her narrow knee. Suddenly he felt water on his face and turning in surprise saw that Emma was laughing silently, the water pistol in her hand.

He wiped his face with the back of his hand. Her laughter burst out.

"Why did you do that?"

"I thought you'd laugh."

"Why did you?"

"Oh, for God's sake!"

"What am I supposed to do now?"

"Dry yourself. . . . I'm sorry, but it's all over your face."

"You put it there."

She took a Kleenex from her purse and roughly wiped his cheek.

"I wasn't thinking," she said. "I loaded it up before we left. It doesn't really work very well."

"You must have been thinking then."

"Of nothing . . . nothing."

"It startled me."

"I can see that."

"It was the last thing I expected."

"I didn't even know what I was going to do with it," she said; then, impatiently, "The hell with it. I'm sorry."

"All right. I'm sorry too, that I got angry."

"Were you?" she asked. "Angry?"

By then they had reached the driveway. Ahead of them was their house, the living room glaring with light.

"Did we leave the lights on?"

"I don't remember," George said, remembering clearly that he had turned them off. "We really need curtains."

He preceded her through the dark kitchen and into the living room. Ernest lay on his back on the sofa asleep. There was a note on his chest; a corner of the paper had been stuffed into a buttonhole of his shirt. "My father locked me out," George read. "I'll go early. Thanks."

30

George stared down at him. For a moment it seemed to him the boy was dead, marked like an unidentified corpse of a disaster. Then he heard him breathing. His presence, his breath and weight and odor filled up the room. The sneaker-shod feet were crossed fastidiously and protectively. Astonished, George felt himself close to tears.

Then Emma pressed the water pistol into his hand.

"You might need this," she said grimly. George reached for the light switch. Emma was standing on the stairs staring straight up. She waited. George went by her and took a blanket from a closet in the spare room. Then he went back down, passing Emma again on his way, and covered Ernest with the blanket.

She didn't speak until they were lying side by side in their bed. "Now what?" she asked, and moved away from him. He had the impression she was propping herself up on the edge of the bed with one hand on the floor. He drew a deep breath and released it slowly. He didn't know what next.

Wasn't Ernest appealing to him for salvation? He smiled in the dark at his presumption. He shifted his position as quietly as he could, as though there were a hostile presence in the room and his only safety lay in silence.

In the thick dark—there was no moon tonight—he opened his eyes wide. Where was the little boy now? Asleep in his helmet? Was the red-headed woman watching him from a doorway? And the blind man? Why did he keep on living? Did the blindness itself give him a purpose?

"George?" whispered Emma.

He turned away from her, shaping and hardening his purpose. He heard Ernest move restlessly in his sleep below. He closed his own eyes.

Chapter Two

FROM sleep he passed directly into wakefulness. He saw the sky through the bedroom windows. It was infinitely pale. It seemed to be balanced on something—or nothing. He felt as though daylight had entered him.

Emma had already risen. A pink Kleenex lay on the floor. Fixing his eyes upon it, he rose slowly. It was when he was standing, about to pick up the tissue, that he remembered Ernest.

But Ernest was gone. The blanket George had covered him with lay on the floor next to the couch; the crumpled note was on the table.

"He ate an apple," said Emma from the kitchen. She came to the door to show him the core, holding its stem between two fingers. George folded the blanket.

"Aren't you going for the paper?" she asked.

"Let's try living without it this week."

32

"I can survive . . . it's only the puzzle. Are we out of coffee?"

The hem of her robe was uneven. He smoothed the blanket and looked at her bare feet. The fiction that she made breakfast every weekday had led to an assumption he was to make coffee on the weekends. She wanted coffee so that she could begin to smoke. Her feet had a grayish tinge. His glance traveled upward. She was leaning forward slightly; her mouth looked drawn. They confronted each other's stare. He strained to name the awkwardness between them at that moment. It required a word. Stuck to the floor, trapped, a frayed blanket in his arms, speechless and in an agony of indecision, about *what* he couldn't fathom, he plucked fuzz. She blinked.

"Did you see how peculiar the sky looks?" he asked, surprised that his voice didn't belong to someone else.

"It always looks peculiar to me."

"Like a pearl," he said. "The way a pearl looks empty. . . . Go sit down and I'll fry you an egg. Go on. . . . You look as if you didn't sleep much. We'll get the paper later. All right?"

She nodded gloomily. "Smile!" he commanded. She showed her teeth.

It would have been a Sunday like any other, but it was not. Emma's despondency deepened. George stumbled into furniture and between one room and the next forgot what he was looking for. The hours lumbered on. He wanted to bathe, to sleep, to find himself immured in Monday.

But he blamed himself for this sad day. He had been ambiguous about Ernest. It was simple enough. Didn't he always withhold from her an essential piece of information? Wasn't that why their skirmishes took place so far from the battlefield? He felt himself staring at her with the tension of one who gauges the listener for tolerance. Words formed into sentences, made no sense, and fell away into incoherence. He sat doing nothing, despite the increasing urgency he felt to face Monday with his class preparations done. Emma unpacked another box of books resentfully, letting them slide to the floor.

She fixed lunch, eating a slice of tomato as she watched him stuff himself—he feeling an uncontrollable urge to appear as gross as her look told him he was. Soon, he thought, she would talk about money or remind him of the paint he had not gotten for the kitchen or, with studied indirection, attack Lila and his concern about her.

You light a match and the house burns down, he said to his reflection in the bathroom mirror, then cut himself with his razor. The small piece of tissue he stuck on the cut remained most of the day until Emma, with an angry smile, poked at it with her finger.

"What the hell is wrong with you! Say it. . . ."

"Say it, say it . . ." she repeated stonily.

"Or cut it out. . . ."

"It . . ." she said.

"Emma . . . please!" But he couldn't say it either. Ernest's shadow lay between them as heavily as though it had substance.

Later that afternoon he tried to make love to her. He had thought, seeing the late afternoon sunlight which lay in warm pools on the green quilt, that they could exorcise the devil. She undressed herself carefully with no more art than a self-righteous child and lay down across the bed, a human sacrifice. Although she didn't look at him and said nothing, he felt an edge of fear as though she might do him physical harm.

Feeling unlovely and overweight, he fell down heavily at her side. She began to weep. It was a blessing. He stroked her gently. With an emotion of relief, without desire, he held her until she was quiet.

"I'm interested in Ernest . . . you know? In school, something has worn away . . . if it was ever really there. . . . A sense of possibilities. It's hard to say. I don't know yet myself."

"Ssh!" she whispered. "Don't talk!"

Was thought possible without words, he wondered?

There was a crisis in school that week. A student asked Harvey Walling to sign a petition to the United Nations asking for censure of the United States for its policy toward Cuba. Walling tore up the petition and dropped it on the corridor floor at the student's feet, then made him pick it up. Minutes later Larry Rubin, author of the petition, sprang upon Walling as he walked by Rubin's office and, according to Walling, tried to strangle him with his own necktie.

Most of the faculty pretended they had heard nothing about it. An English teacher, Helen Finney, said to George that the school was deteriorating when two teachers grappled in the halls over such matters.

"Are we beasts?" she asked softly, her voice swaddled in her thickish lips. She was wearing a knit dress of an industrial red. George smiled because she looked more mineral than animal; there was a stony look on her old girl's face, except for that smooth, swollen mouth. Although George had known her for six years, he had observed only certain surface changes—a growing predilection for violent, unsuitable colors in her dress, the thinning of her soot-colored hair. Unmarried women. But would she have looked any different if she had married? Did he *know* her?

"Someone ought to be reprimanded," she said, her voice faltering. She fiddled with the bow of her dress; one loop was twice as large as the other. Mirrors lied; she probably hadn't noticed. He realized he was staring at her and that she was nervous.

"It'll die down," he said. "People pretend to be more excited than they are, don't you think?"

"Less," she said with unexpected severity. "You're quite mistaken, George."

At lunch Rubin hitched his corded belt onto his prominent hip bones, sat down with a crash and deposited his argument on the table between the meat loaf and the canned fruit. It was imperative, he said, that students be involved in issues—they lived in this world, didn't they?

"No, they don't," Caslow, the Latin teacher, said calmly. Rubin thrust his fork into a piece of meat loaf. It fell back to the plate just as his mouth opened to receive it. George observed that his tie was crooked. He'd probably yanked it around deliberately in front of a mirror. It was an ideological necktie. Impatient with himself, George got up and left the table. Why was he so absorbed in the minutiae of personal dress? Everyone he had looked at that day struck him as being utterly alone, figures hung in space. Did he really imagine, though, that all these people existed only in the mirrors with which he had furnished their rooms? How would he know? Except for Caslow, with whom he shared a small office, he had hardly made a real friend in the school.

"That awful fellow and his revolution is not the best cause for our children to identify with," Ballot said to George later in the day, adding that Castro would be more winning if he would shave. A beard was as much of a uniform as a uniform, and, personally, he was against all such symbols. He must have tried out his view on Rubin, for Rubin told everyone he could collar that only the blackest reactionary could see in Castro's beard anything but the most innocent of human vanities.

At the end of the last period, Walling walked into George's classroom. It was the first time in the three years he had been teaching in the school that he had given George more than a passing nod.

"I'll have that fellow's chops before the year is out! What do you bet he's still paying dues to the party?"

George, bemused by Walling's attentions—if they could be called that—didn't answer at once.

"Well?"

"The children like him," George said, finally.

"He molested a senior girl last year."

"Who believes girls of that age?"

"I do," Walling said. "Every lying one of them." He picked up a volume of poetry from George's desk, then dropped it without looking at the title. "I detect a certain sentimentality in you," he said. "Let me tell you, I'm not against political action. I don't believe in it, of course. But I'm not against it! But let me tell you . . . when I see these fat-brained, overindulged, characterless sacks who think they've got the world by the balls . . . who graduate from Little Golden Books to political causes without shifting their buttocks . . ."

"Jesus!" George exclaimed. "They're children, Walling!"

"Eagle droppings!" Walling said. "Rich kids!"

"What the hell do you want them to do?"

"I want them to learn Latin and Greek and trigonometry. If they are very good, someday they may learn something about human rights. You mistake literacy for enlightenment. Fat brains . . . fat thoughts. A little modesty for Christ's sake, a little leanness in the head."

"Give them time," George said.

"There isn't any time," Walling replied. "Rubin is just the man to finish them off altogether. He'll not get his contract this year if I have anything to do with it. Ballot is not so dumb, you know—not for his purposes, anyhow. Rubin doesn't have tenure! Let him stir up a hornet's nest somewhere else. He'll find some addled old women to protect him. He'll harry some third-rate school to take him on so they won't be called square. And they'll detest him more than we do."

"I don't detest him!" George shouted suddenly. Walling glittered like a cat.

From time to time during the rest of the week, George discovered Walling watching him covertly as though making up his mind about him. But by Friday he seemed to have lost interest in George and he sat in the common room looking at no one, stroking the suède nap of his red vest. George told Caslow about Ernest, leaving out the circumstance in which he had found him. Caslow nodded and said no wonder George was interested in someone like that. "There's something flabby about teaching in a place like this," he said. "If you don't have to exert yourself seriously once in a while, you begin—or at least I do—to feel like a headwaiter leading people to the second-best table."

George quoted Caslow to Emma, but she was silence itself. He dropped it. Don't make waves, he told himself. If the atmosphere was not warm, at least it was neutral.

He met Rubin several times in the corridors and dining room, and Rubin spoke cordially to George as always. George felt a twinge. He ought to have defended him with more feeling. On Friday there was a brief meeting. When notes were compared, it was discovered that cheating was so prevalent in the upper grades, especially in the science courses, that it was a question whether anyone was working at all except for the valiant few who provided other students with answers. Only Walling turned in a clean report. He did not appear at the meeting but sent a note: "No one cheats in my classes because I do not permit it," it read. Ballot waved a copy of the school newspaper. It was a special issue, designed, said the editorial on the first page, to soothe the delicate sensibilities of the faculty. There followed a rambling discourse on the difference between judicious and injudicious borrowing.

Ballot said they would have to institute the use of monitors.

"For God's sake, let's call cheating cheating!" said Caslow.

"I would consider that a defeat," Ballot said reproachfully. Nothing happened at all.

On Friday George called Lila to see if she wanted to come up with him that afternoon but she said she couldn't possibly get ready in time. They would come up Saturday morning.

"Have you had any luck?" he asked.

"Recently?"

"What the hell is the matter with everybody? Jokes everywhere I go!"

"I'm sorry," Lila said mildly. "I was trying to be funny. I didn't get a job yet. I thought you were asking around in the school." The phone banged, then a child's voice screeched in his ear. "Hello, Uncle Beany!" it said. "Uncle Greeny, Uncle Stupid . . ." There was a muffled shout.

"Claude is feeling lively," said Lila. "Sorry, again."

"I didn't ask, because I didn't think you were really interested," George said.

"Listen, we'll talk about it tomorrow. Can I bring anything?"

"Nothing. There's a good train around ten."

"All right."

"I'll meet you then."

When he replaced the phone, he heard a knock on the door of his office. Upon his "Come in," the door was flung open. Henry Sheldon, a junior, stood there looking at him with an expression of insolence mixed with uncertainty.

"Do you have a minute, sir?"

"Just."

"I wanted to ask you about my paper."

"What about it?"

"I think, sir, it deserved more than a C."

"You're entitled to think that."

"I showed my paper to some people—"

"And they liked it better than I did?"

"They thought your mark was unfair. A friend of my father's who's a newspaperman said it was worth at least a B."

"One can't please everyone, Henry."

"My mother is upset, sir. She's worried about college. You know. I'm having a hard time in math, and she says if I don't do well in English, I won't have a chance."

"A chance for what?"

"Oh, come on, Mr. Mecklin, you know what for!" Henry

smiled. George had the vague impression that Henry was about to show him a pornographic picture.

"You'll have to do better to get better grades," he said.

"But what I said about Lawrence was exactly what you said."

"You did not read the novel. You based your paper on my class lectures."

"What do you mean, I didn't read it? I did read it! How can you say that? I mean, you know . . . how can you—"

"You did not read that book. You squirreled together whatever you could remember of what I said. You read a plot summary somewhere. Then you wrote that indescribable hash! The truth is, Henry, I overmarked you!"

"Listen . . . I've got to get a better grade!"

"Not this time."

"What makes you think your opinion is better than a newspaperman's?"

"I have a train to catch."

Henry suddenly smiled. He leaned back against the wall, holding his term paper in his hands. His smile broadened until his protuberant teeth glistened between his lips. George put on his coat and picked up his briefcase.

"I have to lock up," he said. Henry pushed himself straight with his shoulders and took a few slow steps out the door. Then he turned to look directly at George. A tear ran down his cheek and dropped into his mouth. All at once he struck himself on his cheek with the rolled up paper, turned and walked rapidly away down the corridor.

It was too late to take the subway. George took a taxi to Grand Central Station which, as he ran through it to catch his train, boomed and echoed around him. Exhausted, he fell into a seat by the window. He woke into a blaze of late sunlight falling onto the green baize seats. The conductor's hat bobbed in front of his eyes as the man shook him gently. "Harmon. Harmon," he said.

In the parking lot the cinder-and-gravel-strewn ground looked liquid. Beyond the trees a flamingo-colored sky soared. George took off his overcoat and threw it in the back of the car. It was almost warm. Soon it would be April; then he would have a week's vacation.

He slumped into his seat and turned on the ignition. Had he been wrong about Henry? Wasn't it possible he had read the novel and not understood it? They shouldn't read Lawrence at that age, probably. "What makes you think your opinion is better—" Henry had said. "My God! I let him say it!" George said aloud. *"I let him!"*

He saw nothing as he drove home but his own folly. It seemed to him now that he had acted the fool with Walling. Didn't he secretly agree with him? Would he seriously engage a fourteen-year-old in a political discussion? Didn't he hate the unearned complacency of the students? Hadn't he ridiculed Rubin along with everyone else? Didn't he envy Walling his authority over his students? Henry would never have presumed to discuss a mark with Walling.

He was so immersed in his thoughts that he walked through the kitchen and into the living room without raising his eyes from the tops of his shoes.

"George!"

There had been something malevolent in the way Henry struck himself with his own term paper. It was a kind of curse—

"George, your pal was back today."

He looked up to find Emma sitting near the window, a cup of coffee within reach on the sill. Her legs were crossed stiffly. He was startled by a wordless impression of hardness.

"I'm tired," he said, thinking, she's trying to hex me with her legs. "It's been a rough week and a bad day." He set his briefcase down on the card table, flung his coat on the couch and sat down across from Emma. The rigorous lines of her legs softened. "Ernest?" he asked.

She nodded. "It took a while to get rid of him. George, I was scared."

"Of what?"

"You don't sound as though it mattered," she said sadly. Was she sad? He cared about that . . . but did he care enough to find out? To extract bits and pieces of the truth and fit them together so that she too could see she was not sad? So, he didn't believe her, he thought.

"Do you want a cup of coffee?" she asked.

Grateful for any offer, he said yes quickly. With a sigh —for him or at him?—she got to her feet and went to the kitchen. When she returned, she handed him a half-filled cup.

"That's all that's left," she said.

"What did he want?"

"He was looking for you, he said. He hung around all day staring at the house like a haunt. Every time I looked out the window, there he was looking in a window, white-faced, awful! I told him you wouldn't be back till late. He offered me a cigarette when I went out once. I slammed the kitchen door so hard the key fell out. This damn doll's house . . . I felt he could reach in and stuff me into a closet. Then I started to wash the dishes and he tapped on the window and pointed to his cigarette. I lit a paper napkin and opened the window and shoved it at him. He laughed so hard, George, he fell on the ground."

43

"You could have given him lunch. You could have lit his cigarette. You could have acted your age."

She screamed then. "God! God! You're never on my side!"

"I am. And stop screaming, for Christ's sake! You've made him into a menace! He came to see me . . . instead he found an outraged baby! I don't want to talk about it—not now, Emma." He went slowly upstairs.

Later, she came and stood at the bedroom door.

"You lied," she said calmly. "In your usual way. You left out a thing or two, didn't you? He was in the house that day when you found him. Mrs. Palladino said she saw him go into the house when I went out for a walk. She thought we knew him. If you hadn't lied, I wouldn't have been frightened."

He couldn't argue with that. He said he was sorry. She shrugged. Maybe he'd let her in on his plans sometime, she said. . . . How had she come to speak with Mrs. Palladino, he asked. Grudgingly at first, she described her visit.

As George drove off that morning she had stood with her arm around a tree trunk. She was so sleepy, she said, she could have sunk to the ground. The Palladino house shone in the sun, she said, white and still and empty-looking. A door slammed and Mr. Palladino soon appeared, walking up the rise to the garage.

"Ah . . ." he sighed. "It's getting warmer, isn't it?"

There was a long scratch on his cheek. He said nothing to ease her attention away from it, standing in front of her somewhat humbly while she stared at him. His thin hair looked like a doll's. He appeared to be intensely preoccupied. She asked him if he were in some play at the moment. He showed no surprise that she knew he was an actor.

"Brecht," he answered. "I'm tired of it already."

"Still, that's wonderful . . . to be working."

"It's only a studio project," he said. "I don't get paid." He smiled and saluted her with a finger to his forehead and went into the garage to get his car. She felt foolish standing there and waving good-bye to him. When she could no longer hear the sound of his motor, she started for the house, oppressed by the sense of all she had to do, things she had put off since their moving. Today she had determined to take care of everything. But no sooner had she resolved to attack the floors with a scrubbing brush than she thought of the condition of the furniture. It was always that way—resolution followed by dissolution. Then a window opened in the Palladino house and a rag doll was thrust through the opening by a small hand. There was the sound of a slap, then a child's outraged cry. A second later Mrs. Palladino appeared at the window, her hair straggling down the sides of her long face. Imperiously she beckoned to Emma.

The word "please" came faintly from above, a weak gurgle that seemed to have no connection with the ravaged-looking woman. Two small heads inserted themselves in front of her, and stared down at Emma with round eyes. She had been so curious to see the inside of that house, but she hesitated. Then she picked up the rag doll and held it up. But the window was closed. She walked to the back door and waited. When no one came to let her in, she pushed it open and found herself in a dark, cool kitchen which smelled of pickles and whiskey. The two little girls and their mother were standing near the stove, their arms intertwined. Emma let the doll drop on the oilcloth-covered table upon which lay the remains of an anarchic breakfast. A dozen plates crowded the surface, and among the scattered eggshells were bottles of seasonings and sauces and many coffee cups. One of the children giggled; Emma saw they were both naked. The elder child bounced over to the table and seized a huge wet pickle which she began to nibble. The other laughed and hopped from one foot to the other, shaking out her long tangled hair. Mrs. Palladino stepped out of the corner and touched Emma lightly on the arm.

"Stay," she begged. "I have a terrible machine that makes twenty-four cups of coffee. We live on it for days on end. It was a wedding present. I can't seem to make less. You'll have a cup with me, won't you?"

The living room was as turbulent as the kitchen. Empty bottles, clothes, plates and books, toys and shoes, rags and fruit cores, boxes, a hairbrush, denuded spools, a can of dried white paint with a dead fly caught in the skim, crusts of bread and several theatrical newspapers lay in heaps and drifts everywhere. An uncontrollable hilarity rose in Emma. Gasping out apologies, she laughed openly. The children laughed too, flirting with her as they picked their way artfully through the room while Mrs. Palladino, sitting amid a pile of clothes, smiled too, somewhat painfully.

"Sheila is always throwing things out the window," she said. "And I don't go out of the house if I can help it."

"I don't know what's the matter with me," Emma said in a choked voice.

"Nothing. It's nothing. Don't stop," Mrs. Palladino said

wistfully. "There's little enough to laugh at. Mary, go and get some coffee for us." The older child, who looked about seven, had found a wool skirt somewhere and was buttoning it around her waistless middle. She bowed solemnly to her mother and went off to the kitchen.

The two women looked at each other. Mrs. Palladino drew a crushed pack of cigarettes from under the heap of clothes and offered one to Emma. The fit of laughter had passed.

It was apparent to Emma that her hostess had been at some time in her life a beautiful woman. She was tall and thin with flat round breasts showing faintly through a worn blue robe. She was barefooted, and her long, thin legs ended in unprecedented lengths of bony feet. Her hair was of uneven length, of an indeterminate brown color. Her face was hardly lined except for two deep channels on either side of her narrow nose. Beneath thick eyebrows, her deep-set eyes stared outward with a distracted ferocity. There was nothing pretty about her, not her thin bony hands, nor her girl's long arms. But her exhausted face had authority.

"You'll stay a bit? I'm trying not to drink."

"The children are so pretty," Emma said quickly. "Both of them."

"I've been trying for a week," Mrs. Palladino went on as though Emma had not spoken. "I wanted Joe to stay home today. The children aren't enough now. One constructs such a fine balance, you know, very fine, matchsticks in fact. . . . I've thought about these things for a long time. I suppose everybody except me knows all along that guilt is just another out. I only discovered it this morning. You're smiling. Don't feel awkward. This room is funny. It's really deranged. I've considered setting fire to the whole outfit."

"You must have a great deal to do," Emma said, wishing she had left the doll at the back door.

"This morning I wanted to kiss Joe when he left. I stumbled over something and it turned out to be my glasses. I broke them. Then he started to cry. We all cried. I had forgotten, you know, that I wore them. Awful . . ."

Emma grabbed the cup of coffee Mary held out to her and drank it down.

"Have you been to a doctor?" she asked, giving up the pretense that there was anything else to talk about. "They have ways now—"

Mrs. Palladino waved their ways away. "For some. Not for me," she said. "I've been afraid to go out of the house since you moved in because just a week before that, I passed out on the road . . . in a ditch. A bastard we know told Joe she had seen me there and he came to get me." She paused, looked at the cup in her hand and set it down on the floor. "Would the doctor tell me the truth? How could he? I can't find it myself. Every time I turn around and try to see how it all began, the past reshapes itself." She held up her hands as though fending off something. "No!" she cried. "Why must I blame someone?"

"But that isn't the point—" Emma began.

"I mustn't drink," Mrs. Palladino interrupted. "That *is* the truth. I begged Joe to stay, but someone was waiting."

"He was telling me about the play," Emma said.

"I'm sorry," said Mrs. Palladino distinctly. "You're mistaken. He's not in that production. Well . . . what else is there for him to do? You know, there isn't much to *do* in life once you fall through the surface of things."

She smiled suddenly at Emma. "There's only personal truth," she said. "What I said was only for people like me." She stopped, and looked blankly at Sheila, who was sitting on the floor with a book held upside down in her hands. "Sheila, you've got the book wrong."

"I know it," said the little girl.

"Women like Joe. They fall for him in that between-trains way. He can't help it. It's because he likes to please people. I am upsetting you, aren't I? You see, the trouble is I can't keep busy during the bad hours. . . . That's what most people do, isn't it?" She waited for Emma to answer. "Well, how would you know?" she asked sadly when Emma said nothing. "I mean, they take up the slack with habits, stage business, you know! The clock's mainspring breaks but the hands run on. Don't think I'm knocking it! It's only that I've lost the art. People speak to me, I hear the sound but not the message. What I've got to do—" She stopped abruptly, turned up her palms, looked at them, then pressed them together.

"I'd better go," Emma said.

Mrs. Palladino looked at her steadily. The children had wandered off. Emma felt breathless.

"People narrow to their choices," said the other woman. "That's not the same as changing." She took the last cigarette from the pack. "Here. We'll share this," she said and handed it to Emma. It slipped from Emma's fingers and both women knelt on the floor and began to search for it.

"Joe and his women just give me another excuse," said Mrs. Palladino, feeling beneath the couch. She found the cigarette and sat back on her laundry pile. "That low dog who found me in the ditch likes to tell me about Joe. She only comes around when someone is dying. Minnie the police spy."

"Minnie Devlin? I know her."

"Everyone knows her. She's a universal principle. 'Joe,' she said, 'your wife is in an alcoholic coma in the ditch.' "

"I didn't think she was like that."

There was a shriek from the upper regions of the house, then a child sobbed.

"It's all right," said Mrs. Palladino. "They fight sometimes to pass the time. Like adults. Once, I would have run to them. Once, I thought I had what I wanted. Was it though? We were driving somewhere in the summer. The babies were wrapped in blankets and propped up in back of the car with pillows. We stopped around midnight to warm up a bottle for Sheila. A diner was sitting there in the woods all by itself. The lights shone out into the darkness. Joe came running out of it with a bottle in one hand and a carton of coffee for me in the other. We sat there for a while. Where did it all go?" She stopped.

Her lips worked faintly, as though she were continuing to talk to herself. Emma had stood up then and looked up toward the cottage. Ernest was leaning against the garage door. She must have exclaimed because Mrs. Palladino was suddenly at her arm.

"Look at the way he stands," she said scornfully. "He's transferred his crotch to his face!"

Emma looked at Mrs. Palladino's thin, hard profile. How cruel she looked!

"That's all there is of him," Mrs. Palladino said. She told Emma she had seen the boy hanging around the Mecklin house several weeks before, when Emma and George had, apparently, been out. Her hands twitched sud-

denly, her voice grew indistinct. She called the children—
their names ran together as her voice rose higher and
higher.

As Emma made her way to the back door, the little girls
ran past her, dressed in various bits of clothing. Sheila was
wearing an old brown fedora, and Mary had tied up her
hair with a stocking.

"I'd better go see what he wants," Emma said.

"You'd better get rid of him," Mrs. Palladino replied
indifferently.

"He's George's project," Emma said. But Mrs. Palladino had forgotten her. She gathered the children up in
her arms and kissed them furiously. Sheila's hat rolled
off and landed at Emma's feet. She started to pick it up
but changed her mind and left the house without saying
good-bye.

Standing now by their bedroom window, Emma looked
back down the hill. "You'd never believe it . . . how
strange it was! Listen . . . I almost envied her. Isn't that
crazy? I mean she was so *indifferent*. . . ." She walked
over to the bed where George was sitting.

"You didn't tell me the truth, did you? About Ernest?"

"Do you want to be indifferent?" he asked, looking up
at her. She shrugged. "There wasn't much to tell about
Ernest," he went on. "Maybe I did leave out something."

"What did he say when you found him in the house?
What room was he in?"

"I didn't want to alarm you," George said. "And he
didn't take anything. He was listening to the radio, I guess.
. . ."

Emma put out a cigarette with a nervous hand, then

yanked suddenly at her hair. "It's you who scares me," she said.

"Stop pulling your hair that way!"

"What do you mean—he didn't take anything? How do you know what he might have done?"

George laughed. "The diamonds are well hidden."

"Have you ever studied the windows of a hock shop? An old raincoat is negotiable."

"I searched him," he said shortly.

Her expression told him that he wearied her, that in the face of his obduracy, a reasonable being could do nothing.

"I'm tired of working for a living," he said. "I want to do something more than that."

"Join something then."

"I don't want to join anything. I want a point of view. It could be small, modest, but it's got to be steady. If I can help him—"

"You're doing it for yourself."

"I don't give a goddamn who I'm doing it for. I'll make sure he doesn't come around when I'm away. I'll do that." He stopped talking. The room and Emma with it seemed at a far remove. He could have been alone because at that moment he was happy. It was a triumph to feel happiness so unexpectedly, so brilliantly.

"He came back," he said to hear the words.

"Your toy!" Emma cried.

George didn't answer. He went downstairs to the kitchen and made himself a strong drink. He felt a pang as he noted the level of the whiskey. They'd have to buy a bottle for the weekend. He remembered the emergency brandy his mother kept on a kitchen shelf, up above the plates, the pitchers, the seldom-used vases, up in a dusty region of its own.

Poor Emma, he thought, poor thing. Slowly he went back upstairs.

"Let's not fight," he said. "A little amiability . . ."

"Oh, George, no one is amiable any more," she said.

"Try to understand."

She looked at him levelly. "No. I can't. But let it go. I'll stay out of it."

"He's not a toy."

"All right. He's not then."

A truce at least. Emma wasn't cruel, after all. Impulsive sometimes. When he had first known her, the violent decisiveness with which she judged people had charmed him. For Emma, people were enemies or protectors. Even though the charm had worn off, he sometimes envied her— her sense of others was devoid of the kind of complex and enervating reflections he was given to—for within her limits she was clear while he, he thought, moved in a permanent blur. She thought Ernest was bad. Yes. But that was *why* . . .

They ate at the windmill restaurant and went to a movie in Peekskill. George kept his arm around her or held her hand in his. She was quiet and grave, smoking hardly at all, looking off into her own distances while the gray light from the screen played across the faces of the audience who sat there like the dead.

As they drove home—there was no chill in the air but a sweet, faint warmth like late afternoon sunlight—he kept his hand on her arm and felt a kind of sexual flush rising in him. Then he was sad without knowing why; longing made his throat ache and a curious thought came to him. He wished the love-making were over. She was so still sitting there, her shadowed face unknowable.

He woke up several times during the night and, restless,

went down to the kitchen and made himself a sandwich. It was tasteless; the bread was stale and the cheese mostly rind. Then he walked from one window to another. A light went on in the Palladino house. He thought he saw someone running through a room. The light went out. He went outdoors. Gravel stuck to his feet. It was cool, the winter ebb, and he knew he couldn't stay for long though he would have liked to have slept beneath a tree the rest of the night.

The moon had set early, but the starlight was bright and he could see the limbs of trees, blacker than the sky, standing in a perfect stillness. There was not a flicker of wind, only the black, cool air. He looked up at his own bedroom windows. Behind them began the clutter of his life in the midst of which breathed his wife, curled up in their bed surrounded by their gypsy wagon of things. That was his pile. He had made his pile. It could not mean money for him. If he behaved himself, he was a man who would be paid no more than eight thousand dollars a year for the rest of his working life. When they married, Emma had protested passionately against this self-imposed limitation. But she had given up. She began to speak frequently of her aunt as their last hope. The old lady owned three houses in Fall River. During the summers she ran a cubbyhole souvenir shop on Nantucket. She would die someday, wouldn't she? Emma was her only relative. She was a tough old bird, riding her bicycle in the summer, wearing sneakers, her gray hair in a tight bun. George liked her; it was unsettling to speculate about her cash.

He shivered and went back in. The house was unpleasantly warm. He wanted to go out again. Resolutely he went upstairs. Emma was stretched diagonally across the bed. Taking the extra blanket from the closet, George went and lay down on the mattress in the spare room. It was all right. There was nothing in the room except the bed. Two windows looked out at the sky. It was Ernest's room. Empty.

Why was he so sure Ernest would not have stolen anything? He told me, he thought. He likes to go into houses when the people are gone. Voyeurism? No, it was something else. He closed his eyes, remembering. He had taken a trip to California with an aunt when he was eight years old. He had waked in the middle of the night—in the middle of the whole country—and, peering through an inch of steamy window below the stiff green Pullman curtain, had seen through a mist of steam and snow a village, the kind of village a child might draw. Yellow light lay in slats across the wooden station platform, and at the top of a small incline there was a street lamp around which the snow swirled. Just beyond, by squinting, he had made out a road winding away up and up to a line of dark houses upon whose roofs the snow lay in thick drifts. The mystery of it! The sudden huffing of steam, the muffled shout which sent the train into motion. He had turned his head, his nose cold against the window, until he could see no more, wondering who, what was in those houses. His longing came back to him—to be a hundred people, to have a hundred lives!

He fell asleep, stumbling through a child's landscape of farmhouses with chimneys held up by paths like stilts.

He woke early the next morning. Emma was still asleep, both pillows tossed on the floor. He bathed and made himself instant coffee and stared at the orchard gleaming in the sun. The trees appeared to vibrate as though some underground convulsion were about to erupt. It is beautiful, he told himself, and I can look at it for the rest of my life if I want.

Lila and Claude were standing in front of the station huddled together among shopping bags.

"In a few years," Lila said, "I'll be one of those crazy old women straggling down Madison Avenue with a bag full of old newspapers."

"What have you got here?" he asked.

"A cake. A loaf of pumpernickel. A little Scotch. And some old linen of Mama's I thought Emma would like. I can't use it. Claude wanted to bring his truck. And . . . see that bag? It's books. His. He insisted on bringing them to you."

Claude said nothing.

"Claude, why bring me your books?"

"They're from when he was three," Lila said. "I've never managed to get rid of them. He's a great saver. Like a pack rat. Aren't you, Claude?"

"I want to sit in the front seat," Claude said to his mother.

"You sit in the back. Let your mother sit in the front."

Claude sobbed dryly.

"Oh, let him!" Lila exclaimed. "I don't care."

They loaded up the car and, with Claude leaning forward intently, set off on the seven miles to the house. On the way, George pointed out his private landmarks: the thick-trunked oak surmounted by limbs like antlers; a house like a red caboose off in a field without path or steps, as though a rampaging locomotive had flung it there; the stream which followed alongside the road and was all that was left of the river now dammed up into a reservoir. Looking into the rearview mirror he saw his sister's limp smile and, feeling irritated, lapsed into silence. She leaned forward after a while and folded her arms on the back of the seat so that they lay against his shoulders.

"You always liked scenery, George. Do you remember, when we still had the car, Mama saying, 'Let's motor up to Bear Mountain and look at the view'? You wanted to go and I wanted to stay home in the attic."

"Are there any lizards?" asked Claude.

"Ten-foot monitor lizards in the bottom of the lake," said Lila, waving toward the reservoir.

"He'll believe you," George said.

"No he won't. . . . He likes extravagant stories. Which reminds me, I've got a job."

"In one day?"

"It's hardly a real job. When you called yesterday, I was waiting to hear. There was no point in telling you until I was sure. It's in a bookstore near Columbia. The man phoned right after you did. I'll be on the nine to four thirty shift. It barely pays, but think of the atmosphere! And I can walk there from the apartment. And it's dignified!"

Always self-depreciation, he thought, and it touches anything that touches her. There would be no gain in reassuring her; she would drag whatever he said into her system of doubt. She had arrived so soon at an *attitude* of defeat without ever really experiencing it.

Looking at her now in the rearview mirror, her face in momentary repose, he saw that she was getting older, much older than he had ever imagined her, and he was stirred by the thought of his tie with her.

"I'm glad you took the job," he said.

57

"If you want to call it that," she said.

"Don't talk like that! It sounds right to me. It won't wear you out and you've always loved books."

Lila laughed. "Oh, George! If I worked in a restaurant, you'd say, 'How nice, Lila, you've always loved food'!"

Despite Lila's aversion to scenery, she exclaimed over the orchard in which the Mecklin cottage sat. At first she had thought the Palladino house was theirs, and she continued to look at it through the living-room windows as though it should have been.

Later, when the two women had gone into Peekskill to shop for groceries, George took Claude's stiff hand in his own and they went for a walk among the apple trees. A bristle of pine trees filed across the hill above them. A rusty scythe hung by its crescent blade from a tree branch, and Claude and George watched the progress of an ant as it crawled along the upper edge of the blade, then the lower. George took off his jacket, and his pen dropped to the ground. He searched for it in the hummocky grass around the half-exposed roots of the tree.

"Who's that?" asked Claude.

George looked up to find Ernest watching them from several yards away. On all fours on the ground, a root pressing painfully against one knee, George felt suddenly as though he had been knocked down. He got to his knees, stood up and walked over to the motionless boy. Ernest did not belong in an orchard; he looked out of nature, a being who had no connection with seasons.

"Sorry I missed you yesterday," George said.

"I've decided to come around," Ernest said. "Next week. Is Tuesday okay?"

"Yes. About five. Look, I'll give you our phone number. Then you can call if you can't make it."

"I don't want your phone number."

"Who are you?" asked Claude.

"Godzilla," said Ernest.

"This is my nephew, Claude," George said.

"Maybe I'd come on Friday too."

"Take the phone number. There's no point in your coming here if I'm not home. Sometimes I'm delayed in the city."

"Why am I supposed to call?"

"I'd like it that way," George replied.

Ernest zipped up his jacket, then unzipped it. He was wearing a red flannel shirt; the jacket was a sleazy purple satin, the kind basketball players sometimes wear.

"You know about algebra?" Ernest asked.

"Some. I'd like to call the school. I have to know what's been happening with you . . . how far you got."

"No place," said Ernest, frowning. Claude giggled suddenly and grabbed him by the wrist. Ernest with a sharp upward movement of his arm shook him off.

"Godzilla is an ape," Claude said.

"They think I'm sick now," Ernest said. "If you call them, they'll know I'm not."

"I thought you said you'd dropped out of school," George said.

"That's how I did it—being sick."

"I'm not going to discuss you with them. I have to know what the curriculum is. I don't know what they teach here in the senior year. A private school is—"

"You don't get it!" Ernest said angrily. "I can't even do algebra. I haven't read a book like for three years. Don't you get it yet? I've been going there and they've been pushing, pushing. . . . They want me out! They call me to the office and they say 'blah, blah, blah.' They're crazy to give me that diploma. But they can't now. They could push me up but not out."

Claude was laughing teasingly, trying to catch hold of Ernest's waving arm.

"What the hell's the matter with you? What are you—spastic or something?" Ernest cried.

Claude shrieked with laughter and fell on the ground. "Godzilla!" he shouted.

"Take it easy," George said. Ernest started to walk away. "Wait! Stay and eat lunch with us!" Ernest walked faster.

"Where are you going?" Claude cried.

"Mind your own business," Ernest said.

Claude was hauling himself up an apple tree.

"Don't let him scare you," George said. "He doesn't mean to be so rough."

Claude, slowly sliding toward the ground, his arms clutching the tree trunk, gazed after Ernest's receding figure. There was a soft look on his thin-skinned, small face. Startled, George perceived that Claude was smiling.

While Claude ate his supper of cereal and toast, the three adults drank Lila's whiskey in the living room. The darkness came on to the beat of Claude's spoon as he banged the side of his dish. A star shone in the west.

"It's Venus," said George. "See . . . it isn't twinkling. It must be a planet."

But the women cried him down. "Not at this time of year," Emma said. "If it's anything, it's Mars," said Lila.

Two women make a gang, he thought, but he looked at them with a certain tenderness as, dressed in their party clothes, they held down opposite sides of the couch. They were his two women, weren't they? He laughed inwardly.

He smiled, and they both smiled back at him, more remote than planets.

"Tomorrow is Easter Sunday," said Emma. "Shall I give Claude the chocolate rabbit now, do you think?"

"Tomorrow is better," Lila answered. "He'll want to eat it all at once and he'll get a stomach-ache."

"Don't let him," George said.

"Don't let him!" repeated Lila sardonically.

A door banged at the Palladino house.

"This morning," Lila began, "those two men who live on the top floor came and tapped at my door. Do you know what they had? God! They're always so excessive! One had made the other an Easter hat out of meringue and candied fruit. They said it would make a divine breakfast. So we ate the hat, and they deepened their voices and spoke to Claude in a very masculine way and told him to always love his mother."

"You'd better be careful," Emma said.

"Well . . . they've been nice to us."

"Don't trust them. They really hate women."

"They don't hate me at all," Lila said. "Mothers aren't the same as women."

There was a knock at the kitchen door. It was Joe Palladino. He knew they were going to the Devlin party, he said, and he wondered if they could give him a ride. Martha didn't want him to take the car tonight. The younger child had an earache, and if she had to be taken to a doctor . . .

"Absolutely," George said.

"We can't leave yet," Lila said. "Because I have to wait until Claude's asleep."

"You can leave him at our house," Palladino said.

Emma gave her sister-in-law a warning look.

"He'll be all right," Lila said. "I don't use sitters any more. I don't think he wakes up. I hope not. Not that I go out so often."

"Have a drink?" George asked.

Joe smiled and nodded and looked at the two women.

"A party!" he said. "What's so nice as a party? Even at the Devlins."

"Rites of spring," Lila said.

Joe sat down on the couch between them and the women seemed to shrink slightly. George brought Joe the last of the whiskey. He raised his glass and drank and crossed his legs, then looked from Emma to Lila with a kind of in- genuous pleasure. George, looking at Lila, saw the interest in her face; she uncoiled herself, stretched her slender legs and touched her hair with one hand. Her lifted arm, her raised breast and rouged mouth seemed to thrust toward the man. Something scuttled in George's memory— Lila and he, the dark hall, his mother asleep in her bed, Lila's warm breath and damp hand.

The three of them were talking about the theater. They seemed hectic. There was an endless lighting of cigarettes as they bent toward one another, and Emma, describing her brief theater experience, touched Joe's arm. George saw that Joe was not listening at all; his eyes were strained, his smile was aimless and at the touch of Emma's hand, his face subtly hardened.

"Finished!" announced Claude. He had brought his ce- real bowl into the living room and now he held it upside down so that a trickle of milk spilled onto the floor. Lila sighed histrionically.

"Wipe it up!" George said.

62

"I'll do it," Lila said, getting up.

"No, you won't!"

"You're asking for a scene, George."

"Claude, there's a sponge in the sink. Get it and wipe up the milk you spilled."

The boy held out his arms and let the bowl drop.

"Oh, George!" cried Emma. George grabbed Claude's wrist and dragged him off to the kitchen. He forced the sponge into the boy's hand and pulled him back. Claude sobbed heavily. The others were picking up pieces of the bowl and placing them carefully on a table as though it could be mended.

"Wipe!" George commanded.

Claude fell into a heap on the floor and made loose hysterical swipes at the milk with the sponge.

"Now, we'll never get away," Lila said. Emma glared furiously at George. Palladino had moved to a corner near the windows, where he looked reflectively into his empty glass.

What had he done it for? George asked himself. What good would it do? As quickly as it had come, his rage had left him. But he had to carry it through; he must take Claude upstairs and put him to bed in the camp cot set up in the spare room. He felt a fool, dancing around with his pants around his ankles. The child was crying wildly, the two women looking at George with disgust.

He grabbed Claude and carried him upstairs. The boy lay limply in his arms. He covered him up and pushed a pillow beneath his head. Claude groaned; his legs slipped from under the blanket.

"I'll spank you good! You understand?" But he had no conviction that he would do anything now. Lila ran in and gathered up the boy in her arms. Over her shoulder, Claude looked at his uncle with squint-eyed triumph.

They were late in starting for the party. Claude would not let Lila leave. Emma and George and Joe sat silently in the living room listening to the murmur of Lila's voice. The party weighed on George like an odious chore. Emma's eye shadow had smudged and she stared at him reproachfully from panda eyes. The evening had turned into a waste, a desert. In his clumsiness, he had disrupted everyone's life; brawling with the child, he had turned the others against him. And for what purpose? He thought of Ernest probably walking on a dark street somewhere with nothing to do.

"There wasn't much point to that, I guess," he said at last.

Palladino nodded. "Children are tough," he said.

"My sister makes the common mistake of trying to make up for things she imagines Claude doesn't have."

"Don't we all?" said Palladino mildly.

Then Lila, with a martyr's soft tread, crept down the stairs.

The door was heaved open. A male voice bayed out into the night. "It's for early-morning flack. But the commercial is as dainty as my wife. What we're selling here is a peristaltic muffler."

There was laughter—several voices including that of their hostess, Minnie Devlin, who, at the yawning door, offered her pink quivering mouth, her blinding teeth and her pale yellow halo of fuzzy hair to their widening pupils.

"Come in, come in, come in!" she cried, then cocked her head as much as her short neck would permit. "Where's Martha, Joe?"

"Didn't she call?" he asked.

"No, she didn't call," Minnie said.

"Who's there?" called a voice whose owner shortly made his appearance behind Minnie.

"Our new neighbors and my old, old friend, Emma, and everybody's friend, Joe," Minnie said. Her smile perpetuated itself in the ruffle of her dress open to the finely pleated flesh of her bosom. Her feet swelled like muffins through the open spaces of her suède sandals. Charlie Devlin pushed her aside. He was carrying a Martini pitcher in one hand and yanking at the collar of his white sweater with the other. The collar was a monstrous curve of knitting; his small dark head rested on it like an olive on a saucer.

"Give Charlie your coats," Minnie said. "Did you say Martha was sick, Joe? And who is this wearing mauve, my favorite color? George's sister, of course! I can see it! I can feel it! Charlie, get them drinks. Listen, everybody—"

"Let 'em in, Minnie," said Charlie. The huddle at the door broke up. Feeling larger than life, George walked into the living room. A large man in a pepper-and-salt tweed suit stood in front of the fireplace, his meaty hands stretched out on either side of him.

"I'm Benedict Twerchy," he said. "And I'm here to tell you this country is going to the dogs! Tell them that poem, Charlie. You wouldn't believe it!"

"Ben, honey, never mind," cried Minnie, her jelly-roll laugh sugaring the air. "Let the people have their drinks."

"Where did you find that colored man?" Ben Twerchy went on, a locomotive off its track. "Charlie, how do you *find* them?"

"I've got a nose for culture and happiness," said Charlie. "What'll you have, people? Martinis? Whiskey? Name it. Put on a record, Minnie. Do you like stereo?"

A sullen-faced blond woman in her thirties was sipping Scotch from a tall glass and staring at Twerchy fixedly. Finding himself next to her, George introduced himself. "Maralin Twerchy," she said in response, then forcibly removing her gaze from her husband, she told George to sit down—there was no point in standing if you could sit.

"What have you done now, Charlie?" It was Joe, who handed a Martini to Lila.

"Nothing exceptional," Charlie said, with a muscular smile which flickered off and on all the while he spoke, as though there were a faulty connection in his wiring. He struck George as being barely human; he had looked over his guests without a touch of curiosity. "You ever hear of Cleanth Smith?" he asked of the room in general. "He's a very *in* Negro poet. . . . Well . . . we have this new sponsor . . . antacid product called 'PC.' . . . Smith said he wouldn't speak on a program sponsored by such a low-class product. See? But he didn't object to the tranquilizer . . . that's our other sponsor. We don't call them that. Naturally. They're called *'Sedate.'* Get it? Like in dignified."

Twerchy yelped. George saw Mrs. Twerchy's hands suddenly tremble. She clasped them together around her glass.

"So we upped the price. Of course, he came along."

"What I want to know is how you get all those people," Twerchy said, and shook his head at the wonder of it.

"Minnie knows everybody," Charlie said. "Everybody."

"Do you live around here too?" George asked.

"A mile or so away," Mrs. Twerchy answered. "Ben

writes a medical news column. We have two children. We've known Charlie for years. I go to New York twice a week for my classes. I'm going to get an M.A. and then I'm going to teach."

"Teach what?"

"Ancient history," she said. "It's the only kind I can stand." She sighed as though relieved—as though, George guessed, she could now return to her own preoccupation. It appeared to be that of staring at her husband.

Emma had found herself a corner. George tried to catch her eye, but she was taking an inventory of the room. The tendrils of her hair, the wondering, unsmiling expression on her face made her look childish. She was miserable at the moment, he knew. She was thinking of the advantages she would have if only she were someone else.

"Say the poem, Charlie," said Ben Twerchy.

Charlie had pulled a small table in front of him. On it he was setting out his smoking paraphernalia—an ash tray, a cigar clipper, a cigar in its cellophane wrapper. He arranged these items, along with his drink, rather anxiously, as though he might forget some key element of his comfort. Was he preparing for a hurricane? Unwrapping his cigar, he looked up thoughtfully. At least, he thinks he looks thoughtful, George told himself. Charlie intoned:

> "A bronze clapper in a paper church,
> And me, brass-bound,
> Lead-weighted.
> Old possum, disguised in black,
> About to give
> The Judas words
> Of resignation."

"Now do it with that Geechy accent," demanded Twer-chy.

But Minnie, passing platters of paté and pickled mush-rooms, said, "Hush, honey! We don't make fun of the *struggle*."

"You did twenty minutes ago. What happened?" asked Twerchy, pouting obscenely.

Minnie popped a cracker into his big mouth.

"A poop like that," said Devlin, "who writes crap like that, and he wouldn't have PC for a sponsor. Low-class!"

Maralin turned to face George. He had the feeling she was less interested in him than in trying to distract his attention from her husband.

"Minnie told us you'd just moved up. It's pleasant, you know. There aren't many places left around the city where you can find this kind of country. It isn't like a suburb. You know? There are foxes and deer in the woods. Have you seen the little lake—no, no, not the reservoir—the lake that belongs to Cunningham? He's our landlord too. Well, you must have met him when you rented your place. Or did you see Campanelli, his agent? Cunningham's very old. He came here from Ireland sixty years ago and now he's a millionaire. One of his sons committed suicide. . . . It's always the way, isn't it? Does your wife like it here?"

"It's a big change for her. She's lived most of her life in one city or another."

"She doesn't like it, you mean? One is so alone in the country," she said, speaking with the emphasis of personal dilemma. She finished her drink, then looked at him with-out speaking. What he had thought of as sullenness was perhaps only a kind of concentrated desperation.

"Minnie said you were a teacher," she said with a cer-tain deference. "Do you like what you do?"

"I started out liking it," he said. "Oh—more than liking —it seemed marvelous to me. Now—I don't know." He was suddenly shaken at the memory of how "marvelous" it had once seemed. "Maybe I don't really *teach* any more. It doesn't make a difference," he said.

She took his hand in her own and pressed it. Dramatically, intensely, he loved her for one moment. She released his hand. They were apart again.

"Next week Charlie's starting his Latin-American sequence. The dance, art, Indian culture . . ." Minnie announced in a loud voice.

"What the hell's that got to do with happy people?" asked Twerchy in a truculent voice. "What those people down there need is saturation with those tranquilizers you peddle. Calm them down."

"Officially, they're not tranquilizers, Ben," Charlie said irritably.

"Come off it, old horse. I know the field inside out. You think because they can be bought over the counter they're not drugs?"

"All right, all right. I'll tell you the truth. My idea is one inclusive pill. Bang! Take care of everything at once."

"Something to do away with women," Twerchy said.

"Charlie is doing significant work," Minnie said.

Twerchy lumbered into the middle of the room. "You mean I'm an old whore, Minnie? Because I don't interview cultured coons in my column?"

Minnie's fat arm went around Twerchy's tweeded back. "Oh, honey! You're not!" she cried. "Maralin, you ought to build up this man's esteem!"

"Well, I *am* an old whore," said Twerchy, showing his horse teeth in a menacing grin. Then he planted a noisy kiss on Minnie's head.

"Get me a drink, Ben," demanded Maralin, holding out her glass. Twerchy took it from her hand without looking at her.

A small child in blue pajamas entered the room from the hall. He was a plump, pretty little boy, and he smiled placidly at the company.

"Trevor, baby!" cried Ben. "Look how its grown! Look how big it is!"

Minnie ran heavily to her son, picked him up and hugged him.

"Among my wife's many assets is her strong peasant motherliness," said Charlie.

"Always a salesman," said Twerchy.

Minnie went out, carrying Trevor, who gazed back longingly over her shoulder.

George looked around for Lila. She was standing with Joe by a bookcase. They were speaking rapidly in a way that suggested whispering. She took out a book and opened it without looking at it.

"You want to hear our stereo?" asked Charlie. "It's practically a virgin. We haven't played it much yet."

But Ernest had played it, thought George, and imagining Ernest alone in this room, George felt a curious merriment.

Minnie returned smiling. "No music now. Get the people into the dining room, Charlie. We're ready," she announced.

The table, lit by four thick candles, was laden with food. There were tall wine glasses as delicate to the hand as to the eye, and an assortment of casserole dishes in which food bubbled. Charlie shouted seating directions. The guests sank into their chairs. Napkin-opening, cutlery-rattling and chair-straightening gave the sense of a continuing conversation. George sat next to Minnie. Pouring wine, he spilled some onto her plate, and she exploded into laughter—her personal sound. He placed in its wake a pale smile. He noticed the seams of her dress were torn under her arm. Did he like teaching? she asked. Of course he did, she said, before he could answer.

"Teachers can always get work," Joe said.

Emma looked up. "That's what's wrong with them," she said, "using pencil stubs for nickels."

"Where else can you impose your own opinions?" asked George.

"Where have you been hiding out?" Minnie asked slyly. "McCarthy took care of things like opinions."

"It depends on what they are," George said.

"Real opinions are always against the establishment," Minnie said grandly.

"I don't see how you can count on co-operation from the government if you intend to instruct students in how to destroy it," said George. Adrift with the fevered cheerfulness brought on by gulping down two glasses of wine, he swept the air with his arms. "Come on, all of you! You know there aren't consequences from being against anything! My God! You take a swing at the system, and you find your arm slowly waving around, part of the composition."

"What's he saying, Charlie?" asked Twerchy.

"I mean, there's no way of being unpopular," said George. Twerchy ignored him. Minnie gurgled, holding up an arch finger, then went back to her chicken bone. George felt somewhat overcome by his outburst. He had eaten too much. He sat back and observed Minnie as the bone, held by two fat little fingers, slid in and out of her mouth. Her other hand was pressed lovingly against her breasts as she leaned forward over her plate. She sounded like a boat in a squall. When she swallowed her ears crackled. She dropped the bone and rubbed one hand against the other as though snuffing it out. He heard her breath working its way through layers of clothing. He was eavesdropping. To divert his attention from her secret noises, he asked her if she liked music. He himself had been an inglorious listener in school. They hadn't let him sing.

"Music!" exclaimed Charlie, leaning forward to light a cigar from a candle. "What a question!"

"Yes," George agreed. "It's an awful question."

"I mean . . . Minnie and I have the most fantastic collection!"

"Trevor likes Monteverdi," giggled Minnie. "Charlie. Everyone's plate is empty. Eat! Eat!"

They ate; they talked. Minnie's casseroles were bottomless. The guests grew stunned with food and wine. They could have been picked off with peashooters one by one. Only Mrs. Twerchy refused the more and more and more pressed on her guests by Minnie. Coffee came in a huge enamel pot. Their eyes were riveted to it! Rescue!

"What are you doing these days?" Charlie asked Joe.

"Nothing."

Emma dropped her spoon on the floor and let it lie. Twerchy, extravagant and huge, banged against the table retrieving it. He blew on it fatuously and handed it to her.

"So you're out of work?" asked Charlie.

"We're trying out some things at the studio. You know . . . experimental things. There's a chance we may go on tour in August."

"I don't like Europe," said Minnie.

George laughed. Silence.

"What's so funny?" asked Charlie, his red-rimmed little eyes nearly closed, his expression at once hard and languid.

"It struck me funny," George said. "Such a lot not to like." Why was he crouched in his chair? He sat up straight.

"Minnie cuts through all the crap," Charlie said, chewing on another cigar. "The world is full of crap! You know that?"

"Didn't you like anything?" George asked Minnie.

She spoke through spills and falls and chuckles of laughter. He couldn't make out what she was saying.

"What are you laughing about?" It was Maralin, and she was looking intently at Minnie.

"Why so grim, everybody?" asked Minnie sharply.

"What were you laughing at?" persisted Maralin.

"How would you know what anybody's laughing at?" Twerchy said to his wife.

Minnie rose swiftly and went to Twerchy. Leaning over the back of his chair, she wound her plump arms around his chest.

"What you need is brandy," she said, winking across the table at George.

"I always wanted to go to Italy," Lila said. "I have this recurrent picture of myself, walking across the Ponte Vecchio."

"Dear, you'd have to run across the Ponte whatever it is," said Twerchy, clutching Minnie's hands. "You know those Italians! Anything that moves!"

"The way you talk!" Maralin said distinctly. "The goddamn awful way you talk!" She stood up. "I've got to go home. I don't feel well." Then she slumped, her hands gripping the back of the chair. She looked up at George, her face white, exhausted.

73

They left. Minnie got their coats. Twerchy looked at no one, his head down like an angered bull. Maralin said a weak good-bye to the dining-room ceiling.

Afterward, Minnie brought a tray with brandy and liqueurs. Her voice slid into their silence. "They haven't done that for ages," she said. "They used to fight *publicly*, all the time. Very sick relationship. The children, of course, are seriously damaged. But lovely people. You can see he puts up with a lot. Maralin is hopeless. He's afraid of her . . . awful, isn't it? He's the kindest man, isn't he, Charlie?"

"He needs a woman like you, Minnie," said Charlie.

"Are you giving me away?" smiled Minnie.

A spasm of nausea ran through George's stomach. He was drowning in sauces.

"She drinks too," Minnie said, looking across the table at Joe. Joe stirred his coffee and with a barely perceptible movement touched Lila's arm with his own. Lila looked at him eagerly.

They went back to the living room. The brandy tasted thick to George. The air seemed flat—no more fire in the fireplace; the ash trays were filled; the chill of the night had crept into his bones. He felt gloomy and displaced. He wanted to leave. What kind of way was that to feed people? Assault them with food?

Emma asked, "How's the crime rate around here? George insists we don't have to lock doors."

"Never leave the door open," Charlie said. "Never! I keep a shotgun handy. Clean it every week."

"Trevor never sees it," Minnie said quickly. "He doesn't even know what guns are for. I mean, water pistols are all right, but nothing else."

74

"So you're going to raise a different breed of cat," said Joe quietly. "What is he? Deaf and blind?"

"To the rottenness of the world," cried Minnie. She looked suddenly ferocious.

"We had a visitor," Emma said, staring at George. "An unexpected one."

"Somebody broke in?" asked Charlie.

"According to George, he was just there," Emma said. "According to George, he wanted help with schoolwork. George believes in innocence. I don't . . . not in that kid, a big kid."

"He wasn't big," George said.

"Some local boy, George?" asked Charlie. "You want to be careful. This is a muddy area. Economic backwash. Lots of rough types in these woods."

"How old?" asked Minnie.

The Devlins were watching him intently, as though willing him to talk.

"Around eighteen. Just a boy with school troubles."

"Don't you believe it!" exclaimed Charlie. "How did he know you were a teacher? I mean . . . did he just walk up to you?"

George didn't answer. Lila held out her glass for more brandy. Everyone else was watching him.

"What's his name?" Charlie asked. "I can check him out with the local cops. I'll be glad to do that for you. I know the top people around here."

"I don't want to check him out."

"He may need professional help," Minnie said gravely.

"Who doesn't?" said Lila.

Minnie turned her attention to Lila. "There are some mature people in this world," she said.

Joe said, "Whatever happened to the Coochers? They used to have your house, George. Suddenly they upped and moved. I hardly knew them, but they seemed like nice people." He poured himself more brandy.

"I predicted that situation would blow up," said Minnie, her gaze resting on Lila, who had risen and was walking toward the bookcase.

"I'm interested in your motives," said Charlie to George. "I mean, what do you think you can do about this kid?"

"I'm a teacher. I thought I could help," George replied, thinking, I'd like to kill them all. He looked at Emma, but she averted her eyes.

"I'm sorry to hear about the Coochers," said Joe.

"She could be savage," Minnie said.

"You'd better count your silver," Charlie said to George.

"I don't have silver, just dross," said George.

"When you live with them, all people are savages," Joe said to Minnie, who looked meaningfully at her husband.

"You ought to have listened to the program I did on delinquency in St. Louis," said Charlie. "That would have opened your eyes!"

"I thought you interviewed happy people," said George.

"I do. The social workers were happy."

"Yeah . . . well, I'm happy too," said George.

"What'd you say his name was, George?" asked Charlie.

"I didn't say."

Emma seemed about to speak. She opened her mouth, then closed it.

"And he had a girl in the city, of course," said Minnie to Joe.

"Of course," said Joe. "Poor Coochers."

Lila suddenly spoke from her corner. Her voice seemed extraordinarily loud. "I'm worried about Claude. I'm sorry . . . but he might wake up . . . in a strange house."

"We'll go," said George, getting to his feet.

"They're unpredictable at that age," Charlie was saying. "They'll suddenly shoot up a whole household. When they turn, they turn!"

"Claude is seven," Lila said coldly.

"Claude? Who the hell is Claude?" said Charlie. "I was talking about George's little pal."

"Schizophrenic," said Minnie dreamily.

The guests departed. They fell out into the cold, clear night air. The Devlins, their arms about each other, waved them off from the doorway.

"Jesus!" Joe exclaimed. "I always forget the way they are. Usually they have lots of people and you can get lost. I guess they wanted to take a good look at you, George."

"I bet she sleeps in a swan-shaped bed and wears a soiled ruff around her throat," said Lila.

"That bastard and his low Irish ambitions. I don't know which one of them is worse!" Joe said.

There was no more talk as they drove through the dark countryside, hunched and shapeless beneath the black sky. They dropped Joe at his door. There was a light on in the Palladino kitchen. Emma looked back toward it, leaning out of her window until George pulled her back into the car. She shook off his hand, and he drove into the garage with a harsh grinding of gears.

"What's the matter with his wife?" asked Lila. "Minnie was full of ripe hints."

"She's a sot," Emma said, her voice full of tears.

When they were alone, George grabbed her by the shoulders.

"Why? Why bring *anything* up in that wolves' den? Are you so angry at me?"

"Why, why! So you'd see how other people think about doing salvation work with creeps like that!"

"And what," he said, keeping hold of her, "did you think about the Devlins?"

"That doesn't matter. There's a way of behaving. People can be good or bad. But there's a way. . . . There are certain things everybody except you knows. You. St. George!"

"My God! All I'm looking for is a student! Somebody stumbles into my house . . . suddenly I've got a chance to do something that interests me. I've been bored. Bored sick!"

"With me too?" she asked tearfully.

"Oh . . ." he groaned, and let go of her. He went downstairs to get some bicarbonate. His stomach was upset, his feelings in an uproar. What was he being forced into? What was he saying? He tripped over a pile of books on the stairs, and he gave them a savage kick. In the light from the bedroom, he saw the title of one: *The Little Engine That Could*. He laughed helplessly. There was an echo. It came from Lila who was standing by the window, looking down at the Palladino house.

"You'd better go to bed," he said to her brusquely.

She was smiling up at him.

"I'm sorry it was such a punk evening," he said.

"You're not responsible," she said. "I don't know why you think you are."

But he did think so. He didn't know why, but somehow he was responsible.

Chapter Three

Although the Mecklins had planned to go away the first weekend of George's vacation they were, when the sun went down that Friday, still without a destination.

Emma shivered and turned on a light. The sudden brilliance shattered the cloisterlike shadows of the living room.

"That's a hundred-watt bulb," George said. "It's wrong for that lamp."

"A hundred years have passed," Emma replied, "and still we sit here. Why don't we get up and go?"

"All right," he said.

"All right," she echoed, and stood up. "Where? Why not just get in the car and go? Does north interest you?"

"We can't go more than fifty or sixty miles. I don't want to spend the weekend driving."

She swung away, letting him look at her discontented back for a minute before she went on into the kitchen.

"You have to be back on Monday," he called after her.

"There's nothing much to eat," she said, her voice muffled. He supposed she had her head in the refrigerator.

"We could try the Berkshire foothills," he said.

"Jesus!" Emma groaned.

"Every time I make a suggestion, you invoke the Lord," he said. He looked at his hands in the glare from the hundred-watt bulb. They looked webbed. He splayed out his fingers.

Emma stood in the doorway gazing at him, a smile of irritation on her face. "You don't want to go anywhere," she said.

He submitted to truth. "No, I don't," he said.

She ate a saltine slowly, watching him. When she had finished, she said, "You could have said that before. I'm limp. I didn't really care. Why did we go on so about it?"

"We don't have to go," he said, feeling, after the toothless apathy of the preceding two hours, an energy so astringent he wondered if it were mania.

"But it's the first time . . ." she said. "We've always gone somewhere when we had the chance."

"No. There've been a dozen times—"

"Not like this. You know what I mean!"

"You're souping it up," he said. "It's simpler than you think."

"How would you know? What I think. . . ."

"Ah . . ." he sighed, and, rising, went up the stairs to the bedroom. The straw-covered light in a bedroom corner near the three-shelf bookcase cast a sweet light on the books. His briefcase looked fat and soft like a brown animal. The dark scarred leather, the backs of the books, a three-cornered maple stool with one soiled gray sock on it seemed to exude a kind of tenderness toward him.

80

He must be happy, he thought, standing alone in this sheltered angle of the room, feeling an airiness of body and spirit.

There was a sudden shout from below. "You never bring me flowers!" screamed his wife. "You never bring me anything! What am I? A dead horse?"

He bent over with silent laughter—a dead horse, he repeated to himself—or had she said "whore"? Then he rushed to the stairs and down, forgetting his weak ankles, sliding and slipping into the living room where he bumped into furniture and stumbled so that he arrived at the kitchen door as though a second in advance of a landslide.

Emma was sitting at the kitchen table peeling an orange with her fingers.

"Sorry," she said calmly. "I must be going off my rocker." And she held an orange section out to him.

On Monday he drove Emma to Harmon, where she caught an early train to the city. It pleased him to watch her on the platform below. The day was gray, and she was wearing a light-blue raincoat. She looked fresh and young. With small, deliberate steps she paced the platform with the other commuters, one of them, a creature apart from himself. The days when she went to work at the library were the best times for both of them. The set routine appeared to soothe her. Now and then she bought a blouse or a scarf at one of the little shops near the university. She liked him to comment on what she had bought. She would try different beads with the blouse or make headdresses from the scarves.

When he got back the Palladino car was gone. How silent everything was! But instead of the obscure malaise he usually suffered from when he was alone, he felt exhilarated. He started toward the orchard, where spring itself must be centered somewhere among the apple trees. All Emma had been able to find was a plastic gun. But that was unjust; how did he know what else she had found? Did he listen to her with much interest . . . with charity?

Suddenly, urgently, he wanted to get back to the house. He began to run; he stumbled and at once—an inexplicable division—felt himself both object and observer. A painful embarrassment took possession of the object; the observer smiled without comment. Never before had he experienced such inner silence. Was it always there, covered up by the actions of living? Not until he entered the kitchen did he, in effect, rejoin himself. At that same instant he acknowledged the source of his impulse to run. Ernest might telephone.

But that was unreasonable. Ernest would have no way of knowing he would be at home. But reason played lightly on the surface of things, arranging and ordering after the event. No, he didn't believe that either. It was true that while he and Emma were talking about going away for the weekend he had imagined Ernest coming to an empty house. But the *reason* had not been Ernest but boredom. He hadn't wanted to go anywhere.

As the week wore on, he grew preoccupied with other things and only rarely glanced through the living-room windows down toward the drive. He read a good deal, even when Emma was in the city. He planned his program for the last eight weeks of school with an unprecedented thoroughness. He forgot that curious split he had suffered in the orchard; his life, his thoughts had the grave weight of order.

On Thursday he made an elaborate dinner for Emma. A

little drunk, somewhat disheveled, they had a comic evening; they talked and played and joked, and only once George observed to himself that it was all almost real. With something of a swagger, George brushed aside the matter of the dirty kitchen and pulled his wife upstairs. The darkness of the bedroom, the coldness of her hands sobered him. She is watching me, he thought,—my God! what is she thinking about?—and he thrust himself at her body as though to escape her.

Ernest appeared late the following afternoon. Looking at the kitchen clock, George saw he would have to leave shortly to pick up Emma at the station.

"It would have been better if you'd phoned. I have to leave soon."

Ernest looked at him impassively and leaned up against the wall. There didn't seem an easy place to begin. Finally, reluctantly, Ernest admitted his class had read a play, a Shakespeare play. Which one? He couldn't remember. What was it about? Kings, witches . . . George gave him his annotated edition of *Macbeth*. Was that it? "Maybe," said Ernest.

They sat down at the kitchen table. George asked him to read. He couldn't, he said. He couldn't understand the words. George read.

"It's noise," Ernest said after a few minutes.

"It's a terrific story. Give it a chance."

Ernest laughed. "Witches . . ." he said.

"Next time you come bring me a summary of what I've read. I don't care how short it is. Take the book."

He was late getting Emma and he gave her no reason. She sulked. His vacation was nearly over.

———

Ernest didn't come back until May. By then, in the early mornings, there was an intense heat prefiguring the months to come. The orchards were adrift in a milky turbulence. One Saturday George took his coffee outdoors. He tipped back his head and felt the winter dampness of his bones, the sunlight on his winter skin. The earth felt soft beneath his slippers. Emma might be waking now. Her eyes would open suddenly; without blinking she would stare at the ceiling. Then she would sigh, rise and walk to the window and look out. She would have dreamed. She always did. Yesterday she had dreamed she was circling the reservoir in the car. She couldn't find the road which led home; the circles were tightening—she was driving on water. If she breathed once more, the car would lose its magic and she would sink down to the drowned valley beneath, among the mud turtles and the eels.

He was secretly aggrieved she took so little pleasure in the house, the countryside. She seldom read. Sometimes she walked from window to window, leaning her forehead against the panes. He suspected she was doing it for an effect. But of what? Well . . . she had started a garden but that too had its worry. When it rained heavily at night she would sit bolt upright in bed, clutching the blanket around herself, cursing the rain, asking him why somebody hadn't warned her about planting on a slope—everything would be washed away down the hill! Yet when the peas started to come up, she had thrown her arms around George. What a marvelous trick!

Lila and Claude had come for another weekend. After they left on Sunday Emma was melancholy, standing helplessly in the middle of the living room looking at the papers strewn about, the dirty cups and glasses on the table.

Thinking of Lila, he turned to the Palladino house. As he looked a naked little girl came around the corner from the kitchen. She squatted on the driveway and began to fill a pail with stones. George ambled over to her.

"Are you a stone collector?"

"Breakfast," she said, without looking up.

"You're going to eat stones for breakfast?"

"Of course not," she answered, staring up at him through a flurry of uncombed yellow hair. Then with one movement she raised herself up and ran off toward the back of the house, her buttocks shining. He wanted to run after her, to catch her up, to kiss her. He smiled, and a catbird jeered from a nearby tree. A woman opened the back door; the child pushed by her and there was a rattle of stones as the pail was dropped on the floor.

"Good morning," George said. It was the first time he had seen Martha Palladino close up. She looked at him levelly.

"Good morning, Mr. Mecklin," she said. Then she touched a corner of her mouth with her finger as though she feared there was something on her face that needed wiping off. Suddenly she smiled. He thought he had never seen so charming a smile, so diffident. He would have gone closer, but she slowly shut the door.

He walked back up the driveway thinking about Lila. During that weekend she had asked endless questions about the Palladinos, and Emma, who rarely gossiped—George reminded himself he valued that in her—had patched together Minnie Devlin's stories with her own impressions of Mrs. Palladino. From time to time she looked slyly at George. He supposed she thought she was defying him. It was true that he had felt uncomfortable, although that could be accounted for by the fact that Lila couldn't tear her glance from the big white house. George had been aware of her interest in Joe the evening of the Devlin party. But men and women were always interested in each other, weren't they? But that they would act on it, she and Joe—it was out of the question.

Why out of the question? he asked himself. Perhaps they had already met. He quickened his stride to put distance between himself and trouble—to bury that tremor of fear that the thought of change brought to him. But it did him no good. . . . These things did happen. Things, he said aloud. People having things. He looked back hurriedly at the house and caught sight of Ernest starting up the drive. He was carrying several books under one arm. George was oddly touched when he saw the books were held together by a book strap. Where had Ernest dug that up?

"I couldn't come before this," Ernest said when he had caught up with him. "I had to go out on a job with my father. . . . It took a long time. And I went to school and told them about you. So you don't have to call them now." He held out the strap with the books dangling from it: a second-year algebra textbook, a French grammar—"I don't have to take the French, they said . . . but I brought it anyhow"—a textbook, *The Heritage of the Past,* and George's *Macbeth.*

"I wrote up what you read," Ernest said, holding out a piece of paper. The two paragraphs were directly copied from the act summaries given in the book. George said nothing. Ernest's handwriting was fastidious, the letters skeletal and crowded together.

Until Emma came downstairs they sat at the kitchen

table, the books opened before them. George summarized the story of Macbeth. Ernest listened so attentively that his hard beautiful face appeared to soften. He looked ingenuous. "You're listening," George said.

"It's okay when you tell it like that," Ernest said. George, exalted, knocked his coffee cup to the floor and let the fragments lie.

Later he wrote out a dozen algebra problems. Ernest did the first two without hesitation, then he drew a pencil line across the page, then another, bearing down until the pencil broke in his hand.

"What the hell is that for?"

"It's enough for today."

"You're not supposed to come on Saturdays."

"Did you just remember that?"

"Come on . . . let's get them done."

"No more today. I can't."

"I don't understand you."

"Who asked you to?" Ernest said. "I can't do any more. I forgot everything."

When Emma came downstairs half an hour later George was building a pyramid from sugar cubes while Ernest, his arms in adolescent disarray on the table, watched intently. Emma said good morning to George, then asked if he'd made coffee, her voice stiffening into accusation. She was all over the kitchen, rattling pots with one hand, clutching her robe with the other. He had not noticed before how she squinted when she was irritable. Passionate anger was one thing, but there was a comic side to little thorny rages; he supposed it was because there was a confusion of purpose in them. Still, he apologized when he told her he had finished the coffee. She answered by running the tap at full volume. Ernest closed the history book which had been opened to a photograph of the mummy of a pharaoh.

"I've got to go," he said and stood up, keeping his back to Emma, who had not acknowledged his presence—directly at any rate.

"Do you think you can read the play now? It's important you do some work between the times you see me. I think you could work on that page of equations we started too. And if you'll look over that chapter on Mesopotamia—"

"I already read it."

"Read it again."

Ernest glanced at Emma; she was huddled over the stove, staring at the water in a small pan under which she had turned up a high flame.

"All right. But I won't get it."

"We'll work at it until you do," George said cheerfully.

Ernest gathered up his books and cinched the strap around them. Just before he shut the door behind him, he said, "Good-bye, Emma."

"My God! He's insolent."

"Was it too much for you to speak to him?"

"Didn't you hear the way he spoke to me?"

"You're behaving badly. Back up a minute! You've bewildered him. What do you expect him to do? Beg you to notice him?"

"Next you'll tell me he's a baby stumbling around in a dirty diaper."

"I didn't say that. . . ."

"I'm the heavy . . . bullying a little boy."

"He's growing up rapidly. Next you'll have him a dirty old man."

"Don't you care about how I feel?"

"You don't know how you feel," he said sharply. "That's what manners are for—to keep things going when one doesn't know. Let's start over again. I'm interested in him. He's worth some trouble to me." She began to cry, holding her face in her hands so that her robe fell open. She was dressed in shorts and a blouse.

"You're dressed! Why are you wearing your bathrobe?"

She ran out of the kitchen and up the stairs. George turned off the fire under the little pan in which the water had nearly boiled away. He made a pot of coffee. He sat for a while, his hands folded as he stared at the window. Nothing had ever shaped itself so definitely between them as this antagonism over Ernest. What battles had they ever fought? The nervous bickering that went on from time to time was nothing special. Certainly they were both disappointed, but weren't most people? Wasn't it a test of adulthood—the capacity to bridge the gap between expectation and reality? Did he know anyone who was not afflicted with the seepage of discontent? It was in the air one breathed, that undercurrent of fretfulness, of grievance. Yet nothing bad had happened to them, had it? There was no cause for real grief.

Perhaps if he taught a summer session at one of the special high schools in the city, he would have a few extra dollars to take her somewhere. They had had a good week in Vermont years ago shortly after they were married. One afternoon they had followed a stream for several miles until twilight darkened the woods; how sweet the sound of the water had been in the darkness! Standing on the bank of the stream, he had felt sustained, exalted, by his place in the nature of things, the woods, the unseen life all around them; the energy of the moving waters was his energy too.

On their way back along the dirt road which led to Putney, she had stumbled on a root and, crying out, had sworn there were snakes all around them. He had thought her silliness endearing. What had diminished them so? What had *he* stumbled on?

He would take her coffee. He would sit on the bed and hold her and they would talk.

But when he was there holding out the cup, she was so unlike the person he had been thinking about downstairs that he stared at her fixedly as though trying to place a face he had once seen.

"Don't let's fight," he pleaded with the woman lying on the bed. Her red-rimmed eyes stared back.

"We don't know how . . ." she said.

Ernest began to come frequently, his presence for George inextricably part of the softening of the landscape, the warmth that descended upon the countryside like a mantle of fine fabric. He had been able to help the boy with trigonometry, although it meant giving up a large part of his free time in school so that he could study mathematical texts. Walling, looking over his shoulder in the library and seeing what he was reading, asked him sardonically if he were exchanging the mess of literature for the order of mathematics.

At first Ernest had been capricious, restless, talking rapidly in his low voice about the city people who had moved into the houses around the reservoir over the last few years. Sometimes he spoke like a general scouting out a territory he intended to attack. Sometimes he presented George with an inventory of objects, desired, unobtainable —"Where do people get money? Where, how? More shoes than I had in my life . . . tool kits, shiny, don't they use them? Electric stuff, something to do everything with. . . . Jesus, how do they get it?"

George felt intense pity; he tried to speak to the longing in Ernest, to dissuade him from making a mystery of the economic profligacy about which, as he tried to explain it to the boy, he found himself growing long-winded and uneasy, as though he were lying subtly. But then Ernest would laugh; the tension in his face would be replaced by a loutish leer as he described other things he had seen. George told himself it was defensive—these stories Ernest recited so wolfishly. The scenes were stripped of humanity, like the scrawled graffiti in public places, and George was haunted by them—Charlie Devlin sprinkling his fat, naked, laughing wife with gin; Martha and Joe Palladino beating each other and weeping while the children watched from behind furniture; Benedict Twerchy cursing his wife foully in a voice cracked with rage as he stood in front of her, half-dressed, a newspaper held in front of his child's genitals while she sat reading a book as though he wasn't there. "A big bastard like that!" Ernest had said, shaking with laughter. There were times when George drowned in flesh— its odor, its terrible softness. Ashamed, he slept lightly on his side, a knife on edge. Making love, he and Emma had always called it, and in the mornings their faces were as smooth and expressionless as stones; no witness to confirm what had gone on in the night.

If that had been all, he would have abandoned Ernest to the street. It wasn't. Ernest would like to go to Egypt, he said. He would like to see those pyramids, ancient bones wrapped in yellowed linen, ships of the dead. On a Saturday afternoon George took him to the Metropolitan Museum and Ernest brooded for a long time over the glass cases where the mummies lay encased.

They had finished *Macbeth*—it was more a translation than a reading—and had gone on to *Julius Caesar*. When it came to history, Ernest grew fidgety and irritable. "I'm losing it," he'd say. "I don't hear you. It's just noise." They would stop then—it was such a small flame George tried to feed, perhaps, he often thought, only a reflection of his own—and George would talk. The ancient world was constructed on the kitchen table, a parody, lopsided, its lineaments determined by Ernest's interest. George watched for cues: Ernest's widening glance, his smile, a snort of surprise, a look of disbelief.

He had to convince Ernest of—of what? Convince him that much had gone before, that he had not sprung from sticks and stones to find himself on a dead planet thinly covered with sidewalks leading nowhere. So he permitted himself a kind of freewheeling rearrangement of the buried landscapes of the old world. Sometimes he heard his own voice and was struck by a force he had not imagined he had, but at other times he choked on the constraint put upon him by Ernest's limitations. He saw himself as a purveyor of comic books. He would speak coldly then. There was no point in studying Greece if you were unable to understand the significance of the polis. There was a right and wrong order, a sequence; there were causes and effects, not only the great thrusts of events.

"Tell me some more about the pyramids, about the slaves who were killed, about the way they put their guts in jars. Tell me about that. . . ."

Exasperated, George would turn to something else—mathematics. Ernest worked well then, as though an impersonal authority was in charge.

92

George began to see that Ernest was too thin, that his nunlike pallor was unnatural. He gave him food; Ernest ate it without interest. Once he asked him if his father knew he was coming to George.

"I haven't seen him for a while," Ernest had answered.

"What do you live on?"

"He left me some money," Ernest said.

Now and then George gave him a dollar or two. He took it without comment, looking at the bills, then stuffing them in his pocket. George felt oddly gratified by his silence. He wondered what Ernest did when he was not with him. He had seen him once when he had gone in to Peekskill for the Sunday paper, part of a group on a street corner. They were waiting around, he supposed, for something to happen, for an impulse, for anything at all. It wasn't hard to recall the boredom of his own adolescence—that suffocating idleness when everything was offered and nothing was given. Standing around, waiting. Still he had felt a pang seeing Ernest there among the others.

Yet he was sure Ernest was changing. He no longer told him what he had seen through other people's windows. At first, George spoke of how morally distasteful it was, but that had gotten him nowhere. Ernest had grinned. Then he spoke of the risk Ernest took. Ernest shrugged. But he stopped.

One afternoon he interrupted George as he was explaining the conspiracy against Caesar. He said he had watched a beating the night before. No, not through a window. He and some friends had caught a colored boy.

"Why did you beat him?"

"He was too black," Ernest said. "I watched. I didn't touch him."

"You liked watching?"

"Yeah, I liked it. He was too goddamn black."

George looked at him in silence.

"You look so *refined*," the boy said and burst into laughter.

"I could turn you in for that."

"No, you couldn't. I made it up."

"I can find that out too."

"Jesus! You look funny!"

"Get out! Come back when you can behave."

Turning over his chair, still laughing, Ernest ran to the door as the chair clattered to the floor. He hesitated, his hand at the door.

"I have to go. That's all for today anyhow."

George began to pile up books.

"Come on! Don't be sore. I wanted to get a rise out of you."

"You did," George said.

"I'm sorry," said Ernest. Startled, George turned to look at him. He was not laughing. "I'll pick up the chair," he said and walked back to the table, righted the chair and looked intently at George.

"All right," George said. "But no more of that. The world is rotten enough."

"Rotten," echoed the boy, and with a nod was gone.

Emma was standing in the doorway. She looked at him without speaking. She walked through the kitchen to the refrigerator and opened it.

"I have to shop tomorrow. Is hash all right tonight? We're about out of everything."

"Fine."

"What was going on in here?"

"I've been pressing him too hard. He got sick of listening to me."

94

They had not spoken about Ernest since her outburst that first Saturday in May. He did not imagine she had changed her view; it had gone underground. Except where it was unavoidable, they had skirted the whole subject. If she needed to use the kitchen, she would ask him to work in another room. And with some vague idea of reassuring her, he had taken Ernest to the museum only after Emma had made arrangements to visit Minnie Devlin. Still, the sharper edges of her disapproval must be wearing down if only because that is what happens in life; in the end you learned to live with things once you stopped talking about them.

He didn't want to start anything, but he wanted to talk about Ernest. He studied her. She was slicing a tomato, her fingers barely touching it, holding the knife gingerly in the other hand.

"Do you want a poached egg with it?"

"Yes."

She sighed and yanked open the refrigerator door.

"I think I've got him interested," George said. "For the first time in his life . . . in things outside himself."

She cracked an egg and spilled it into a saucer. Then she handed him a can. "Can you open this? The opener sticks. We'll have to get a new one."

"I've just begun to realize that the capacity to be interested is a luxury, you know? It gets handed down—like property. People like Ernest have no heritage of that interest."

"Don't bother," she said in a flat voice.

"What do you mean? I'm trying to tell you something."

"You won, didn't you? Do I have to join the club too?"

"I had no idea you were so bitter about it."

"Oh, but you do! That's the worst of it."

"I'm not so sure I know anything about you."

"Don't start up with that. I can translate for you—what you mean is you think you know everything about me and you don't like it."

"I shouldn't have brought it up."

"That's right." She flattened the hash into the frying pan with a spatula. He observed that her face was broken out around her mouth and suddenly he remembered Mrs. Twerchy's splotchy chin and the way she tried to hide it with her hand. He went up to Emma and put his arms around her.

"The exams will be over soon. Let's go away for a weekend. Really. Someone told me Narragansett was nice. Would you like that?"

"Yes," she said. "I'd like that. Can we afford it?"

"No. But we'll do it anyway. What would it come to? Fifty dollars for the weekend?"

"That would be lovely," she said.

She told him then that Lila had phoned during the morning and asked if she could come up for the weekend.

From time to time George stayed in the city until five when Emma was through at the library. They caught the train to Harmon at One Hundred and Twenty-fifth Street. The next day, one of Emma's working days, George called Lila and asked if he could stop by. Could he come to the bookstore, she wondered? She had to work until four thirty.

He took the Broadway bus up to Columbia after school and got off at One Hundred and Sixteenth Street, finding himself among a throng of students, crossing to the subway, to the bookstores, to the restaurants poked into the gloomy façade of Broadway buildings.

Lila was standing in front of a rack of Penguin paperback books. She looked better than he had seen her for a long time. She was wearing a sand-colored jacket and brown skirt, her handsome head of hair done up modestly at the back of her head. There was a subtle difference in her style, a kind of trimness. He was really glad to see her and pressed his cheek against hers in a rush of affection.

"You look like ready cash," he said.

"I'm fine. Look at these books! Doesn't it all look like antipasto? Do you remember the bookstores when we were kids?"

A young Negro man called out "Lil!" and Lila turned toward him. "Did you find Arthur Machen anywhere?" he asked.

"I called all around," she answered. *"The Hill of Dreams* is out of print." She leaned toward George. "Isn't that nice? 'Lil.' I think I'll have my name changed legally to that. . . . He's a darling boy, that one. He's at law school. And he knows every book that's ever been published."

"How's Claude?"

"At first . . . Well, he's all right now. They keep him at school till five. He doesn't like that. George? Listen, I've learned something. You can't talk things over with little kids. The *fait accompli* is everything in this life!"

"Emma said you wanted to come up for the weekend."

"I called. Yes. Are you too busy? It's near the end, isn't it? Final grades and all that?"

"Come up, of course. This weekend if you like."

"How are your neighbors?" She was smiling slightly. He caught hold of her arm and didn't answer, only looked questioningly at her.

"All those people I met—"

"Lila? You're not getting into anything, are you? The Palladinos are in a bad way."

She shook off his arm. "He wouldn't be interested in me . . . hardly!"

She left him standing there while she went to the cash counter and picked up a paper bag behind it

She took off her jacket when they got on the street. "It's getting to be summer," she said. She was wearing a thin sweater, and George saw that she had gained weight. He wanted to ask her about Joe Palladino, but he was afraid of her smile, afraid she would lie in such a way as to let him see the truth. They walked to One Hundred and Thirteenth Street in silence.

"There's Claude," she said, pointing down the street. Claude was standing next to a nun not much taller than he was.

"That's Sister Eulalia," Lila said. "She's a perfect mouse. She says you can cure sore throats by sucking on a cube of sugar."

"Is it a Catholic school?" he asked, surprised.

"God, no! An Episcopal order. Just right for Claude. Very structured, as they say."

"Listen, Lila . . . You know I want you to be happy."

"Happy!" she exclaimed and burst into a brief loud laugh like a cough. "Do you still believe in that old thing, George?"

Four young men walked by. They were disparate in physical type but each face bore the same sullen inward look. They were thin, shaggy, book-carrying, slovenly, and their arms and legs appeared to have been glued on with little consideration for symmetry. "I have seen the future and it walks," George said. At that moment one of them turned and stared at Lila, at her prominent breasts. There was no expression on his face at all. The movement of Lila's hand to cover herself was hardly perceptible.

"It's chilly," George said. "You'd better put your jacket on."

"I guess it is," she replied. He watched her walk down One Hundred and Thirteenth Street to Claude who, breaking away from the nun, ran uphill toward her.

Presently he met Emma in front of the library. She blinked like an owl in daylight. "I've been in the stacks for ten years," she said.

"Let's have a drink before we get the train. That'll restore your sight."

"We'll miss the five twenty."

"There are other trains."

They walked companionably through the stone-hedged campus. How strange it was that without touching her he could feel close to her. Perhaps it was because there were people all around. Perhaps they had done better in the city.

The bar was an echoing chamber lit by cold blue light. The neon tubes which ran along the wall above the booths suggested medical equipment. She wouldn't be fit to cook if she had a Martini, she said. He told her not to worry—they could eat eggs and toast.

"What do you think about Lila?" he asked, and was startled by his own question.

Actually he had been thinking about Rubin, who had provoked another crisis in the school by demanding that the upper forms be encouraged to hold a weekly forum on politics. The first topic, Rubin had said, should be a discussion of Communist China. Walling had said there were a few things left a man had a right to privacy about, and one of them was Red China. Why not have a forum on sexual deviation? That was a proper subject for public discussion. Rubin, rubbery, sweating and outraged, Walling, rigid, cool and vicious, had struck George as being essentially comic; what separated them was not so much ideas as the essential opposition of their natures.

"Where are you?" Emma asked.

"Oh—I was thinking about something that's going on in school."

"You asked me about Lila. That was queer. You've never asked me before."

"Well?"

"I don't know that I really like her. Maybe she's become too familiar by now. She is much older, isn't she? I mean, than I am. I think I can stand her when she's broody, you know, when she gets quiet. It's that breathlessness that bothers me."

"It's inappropriate?"

"That's right. She's nearly middle-aged, isn't she? And she made such an obvious play for Palladino that night at the Devlins. And that seemed crazy. I've thought about him. . . . I have this feeling that he's stuck in some kind of posture, like an adolescent suitor, that he can't get out of. I mean, he'd fall down in a heap of bones for anybody who looked at him." She looked disgusted. "She ought to pick on somebody her own size . . . whatever that is."

Forgetting for the moment the discomfort her words aroused in him, he reached across the table and took her hand, but she withdrew it at once.

"You're surprised," she stated. "You're surprised I had so much to say about her. Do you think I'm only here when you look at me?"

He felt remorseful. He had to acknowledge there was some truth in what she said. Would Lila have reached home yet? He fought down an impulse to telephone her. What could he say? That she must be patient until age freed her from the rack?

"Oh, look!" said Emma.

A small, yellow dog had run into the bar as several people pushed open the door. Its ears were flat, its tail between its legs. It crept through light and shadow to their table, where it lifted its narrow muzzle abjectly.

"Could we take it home? It's lost. Oh, the poor thing. It's got that lopsided way of running."

The dog's tail brushed the floor in a tentative wag.

"We couldn't get it on the train," George said.

"They must have a baggage car. Maybe we could ride with it? Look how its ribs stand out!"

"There's no way we could get it home, Emma," he said irritably. "Come on. We'd better get going."

The dog followed them up to the bar where George paid for their drinks, then trailed after them through the door.

"We'll take a cab," he said shortly.

Emma looked back through the taxi window to where the dog still stood. Reluctantly, George followed her glance. At that moment the dog set off running down the street until it was lost among the crowd.

"I should have just grabbed it and brought it," she said as though to herself. "I could have done that. . . ."

George had gulped his Martini after the dog had come to their table. He felt curdled, as though his substance was separating. He had no business taking a cab. His monthly check was a week away. He and Emma kept separate checking accounts; hers was supposed to go for extras, beyond rent and food and the car upkeep. But it usually turned out he paid for them too. He felt the sharp twist of an unspoken resentment against her and her chaste bankbook.

How long had it been since he bought himself something new? His clothes were so old they hung on their hangers like humble effigies of himself. In her female ignorance, she imagined him indifferent to such things.

The train was crowded, and they were unable to sit together. She was several seats in front of him. He could see the top of her head and sometimes her profile when she glanced across the aisle. He thought about her comments on Lila. Girlish Lila. But Emma was not so much younger. What would Lila have said about her? Did one only know oneself in others? Of course, there were major differences between them: Lila was unbuttoned. She had no secrets. Emma, though, could build up her little bank account with cool perseverance. Or was it so little? Every two weeks she had to "go to the bank." He could see her with her sewing-machine steps running to the savings window, running her eye down the figures. He felt possessed—it was astonishing to him that he could sit there when he wanted to rush down the aisle and seize her and demand to know exactly how much she had secreted over the years. Damned ant!

"I wish we had a dog," she said on their way home from the station.

"You said a long time ago you'd ruin a dog. Now drop it! I thought it was a baby you wanted."

"How? Parthenogenesis?"

He groaned. "Do you imagine your delicate signs of forbearance could warm up anyone?"

She answered him levelly. "No. I wasn't saying it was your fault. But something is wrong, isn't it?"

"Yeah . . . well, what are you saving it for?" But he didn't know whether he was talking about money or sex.

"I guess we can't talk about it."

"Hit and run . . . you knock me down and then pretend you're an impartial observer," he said.

"I'm sorry," she answered coldly.

They had been married years ago at the height of an exchange of confidences when the last, ultimate secret they could share had been contained in his offer, her acceptance. They had been married in a place called Cherry Grove in Pennsylvania.

"It is a truth universally acknowledged," Jane Austen had written, "that a single man in possession of a good fortune must be in want of a wife." But he had had no fortune; at the time he had been in want of a job. Glancing at her profile at once so mysterious and so familiar, he felt as though he had hit her. She *had* touched him; he had *wanted* to love her. "I love you," he murmured aloud to persons unknown.

He heard Emma's astonished exclamation. "Take my hand," he demanded urgently, and took his right hand from the wheel and thrust it toward her. She took it but she had waited an instant too long; their clasped hands were lax—it was not what he had meant at all.

Tonight he must start reports; some would make him writhe with impatience. The school never gave up. Students who failed seemed to be its *raison d'être;* hysterical parents had to be cozened into a patience they could only simulate. "He needs more confidence. . . ." How many times would he have to write that before the day was out? But was it confidence? What about failure? Perhaps old Ballot was right. Neither among those who attained the factitious success of an unbroken file of A's nor among those who endured without hope their classroom imprisonment was learning involved. As for the real scholars, they were invincible; failing or succeeding, they always learned. Ballot said the purpose of teaching was to corral the strays. Lost sheep, Ballot had said. What about Ernest, a lost wolf?

It was dark when George parked his car next to Palladino's old station wagon. He went ahead of Emma to turn on the lights. She passed him on the stairs, looking, he thought, rather pleased with herself. Feeling a kind of meaningless hunger—he had no appetite for anything at the moment—he opened the refrigerator.

"George!"

Hearing the fear in her voice he ran to the living room and started up the stairs, his heart pounding.

"The radio is gone!" she cried. When he said nothing, she repeated, "The radio . . ."

"What about it?"

"I said it's gone."

"Where?"

"It's been taken. And probably not the only thing."

"The radio," he repeated. "All right. I'll go and find him." He fled the house before she could say anything else.

It was several miles to Peekskill. Possibly Ernest might still be on the road. George didn't even know where he lived. He drove down the blacktop road until he came to the turnoff which led to the old emery mine. There he stopped. What point was there in going on? If he found Ernest, if the boy admitted he had taken the radio, would he turn him over to the police? Thinking about what Ernest might do, about what he himself might do, staved off the shame that was more his than the boy's.

Nothing that had happened had prepared him for this. He was not such a fool as to imagine Ernest had never stolen anything. George had seen him pocket a few marking pens, but openly, almost as an act of trust in George.

Sweating there in the dark, his hands gripping the steering wheel, he told himself this was a test even as his pride cried out in protest. Ernest had betrayed *him*. The idea, the rescue—what had he imagined he was doing? Ernest was a thief; his peeping was no simple-minded pastime but a sinister aberration, and he, George Mecklin the goddamned fool, had thought to change him by offering him dead heroes and dead poets.

But he would not call out the police. Revenge was a low act; what did a radio matter? If Ernest never came back, that would be the end of it. At least, George had tried. But there was an end to understanding.

He backed the car around and started for home. Ahead of him in lighted rooms his wife waited. What scene was she composing? Would she feel sorry for him? And Ernest was carrying the radio down some street in Peekskill by now. Would he sell it?

Emma had heated soup and toasted bread. On the bare kitchen table an ant was crawling from one soup bowl to another. Then it felt its way into the folds of a paper napkin. Waiting for Emma to speak, he watched the napkin. When she shook it out, the ant dropped to her lap. He suppressed a desire to laugh as she stood up hastily, looking down at her inviolable self.

He told her he hadn't found Ernest. She nodded without surprise. She hadn't expected him to, she said. But he wouldn't get much for a radio like that—it was a cheap thing.

"Too bad we didn't have something valuable for him," George said. The soup burned his mouth. There would be no comfort here.

"I'm sorry," she said. She sounded genuine, all right. She was sorry for him.

"There's more to it than that," he said.

"I only said I was sorry."

". . . because as things turned out, you were right." It must, under the circumstances, be pleasant to be sorry.

"Have some toast."

"I'd do it again. A hundred times."

"Do you want coffee?"

"Neatness is all. We live on the edge of disaster and imagine we are in a kitchen."

"Who does?"

"All of us. The ones with houses."

"I don't pity him. I don't pity any of them. Things get a little better; they get a little worse. It's as bad in houses as anywhere else. I meant I was sorry because you were disappointed. You think I'm queening it over you because I was right. Who cares? I want to lie down. . . . I'm very tired right now—"

"You weren't right. . . ."

"I am . . . as far as I have to be."

"I can't argue with that."

"No, you can't."

He picked up his bowl and drank the rest of his soup. She was waiting for the plate.

"Go on up," he said. "I'll wash the plates."

She demurred.

"I said—I'll do them."

He cleaned up scrupulously. An ant crossed the floor and

he stepped on it. He wondered if it was the same one. There were so many of them.

Lila came with Claude the following weekend. She rarely strayed from the window which looked out on the Palladino house. It seemed to George she was determined to keep a twenty-four-hour watch. In the middle of the night he had gotten up to get something to eat and, coming downstairs, had found her at the window, a pile of cigarette ends in a saucer on the sill. He tried to bully her into confidences she would, formerly, have not spared him. Now she said nothing. She stared at him pensively as he exhorted her, pleaded, warned her. At the dedicated folly of her glistening eyes, he gave up.

On Sunday morning he discovered her leaning on the Palladino station wagon, her nose pressed against the window.

"For God's sake . . ."

"I know . . . it's awful," she said.

"I know certain things about him."

"So do I. I know them all. What good do you think that ever does?"

How long, he wondered, had it been going on? How often did they meet? Did he come to her at night when Claude was sleeping—assuming that Claude ever slept?

"It's so godawful inappropriate. . . ."

She cried and gasped with artificial laughter. Then she patted his cheek. "There's a lot you don't know, little brother," she said.

Loathing her, he drew back. "Nothing will come of it," he said.

She put her finger to her lips to silence him and they both glanced back over their shoulders at the same time.

The youngest Palladino child was standing behind them, her hand on the taillight of the car. Lila was mesmerized. And George, listening for the footsteps of the hotel detective, heard the crunch of several feet on gravel. His impulse was to grab Lila and toss her into the kitchen. Joe and the older girl came out of the sunlight and into the garage.

Palladino bobbed his head at the two of them as they stood there in the shadows.

"Going for a drive," he said. He grinned into the air.

"Good day for it," said George hoarsely.

"That's a pretty dress," Lila said vaguely, looking at one child and pointing at another.

"Oh, hello," said Joe. "Up for the weekend?"

"Hello," Lila said. Neither looked at the other. The children scrambled into the car. "Come on!" muttered George. Lila, smiling as though he had complimented her, moved indolently toward the kitchen door. Once inside, she made for the living room, where Claude was playing on the floor with a deck of cards.

"Look!" said Lila. They saw Mrs. Palladino standing in front of the big house. She was wrapped in a raincoat that fell to her calves, her head covered with a scarf. She appeared to list slightly to the right. Presently there was the sound of an imperfect muffler, a grinding of gears, and then the station wagon stuttered to a stop in front of her. Joe got out and led his wife by the arm to the other side. Then he opened the door, helped her in, tucking her coat under and around her.

"Like Mother," Lila said. "Like poor old demented Mother on a Sunday outing."

"Mother," echoed Claude from the floor. "What mother?"

Lila ran to him and, kneeling, flung her arms around him. He poked his head through her arms and continued with his card game. She kissed him rapturously.

It was indecent. "You ought . . ." began George.

"What . . ." she said and looked at him through wisps of hair, her eyes sly. He only noticed then that she had not done up her hair. He supposed it was gorgeous, that thick, wild slither down her back. Yet as she crouched there, her arms around the little boy, she looked old and strange. He went upstairs to the bedroom. Emma was lying down, reading a magazine. As he came in she looked up at him coldly and dropped her cigarette into a coffee cup on the floor.

For the next two weeks, George immersed himself in schoolwork. Final grades had to be computed, late papers marked, reports finished. There was a series of meetings which George attended dutifully. Walling made a point of falling asleep—or pretending to. Rubin, who could usually be counted upon to irritate people into some display of temperament, looked enervated and worried.

The post-examination classes writhed in their seats, listened not at all, refusing to be either entertained or threatened. George had lost control of his classroom and he kept as constant an eye on his watch as his students kept on the wall clock. It had never been so difficult. Sitting at his desk, his hand on a closed anthology of poetry—the idea that he would read them poems had occurred to him in the middle of the night, like most fatuous ambitions, he thought—he kept them at bay with short barks of bad temper as they pawed the ground and shook their great adolescent heads at him.

Between classes he brooded over Lila and Ernest. She called once, leaving a message, but he had not phoned her back. He felt he knew it all now—he didn't want to listen to her. Yet how could he condemn her? He was not unaware of her loneliness, of the small, detestable privations of her situation. He knew she would be forty some time this month although he couldn't remember the day. He told himself that, like Ernest, she deserved an especial pity because she had so few inner resources, just because she was inept and foolish. But she might have had the sense to have resisted the stale charms of his only neighbor! He barely spoke to Palladino any more, and the other man with his aimless apologetic smile seemed as reluctant as he was to start a conversation.

George had driven around Peekskill on two Sundays looking for Ernest. The nearly empty streets, the bright morning sunlight of early June and the buoyant gleam of the Hudson River behind the town filled him with despair; he felt purposeless.

His last class, relatively quiet, had left. He went to the supply closet and opened it with his key. A smell of old books and chalk rushed out into the classroom like the released ghost of other winters. For an hour he stored his books, his erasers and blotting pad, an armful of unused blue books and all the other paraphernalia of teaching. It was warm in the room; the silence was a blessing. Lifting the books and piling them up on closet shelves, he felt the softness of his body and he determined he would do something about tennis this summer. There was a knock on the door and, at his shouted "Come in," Walling entered.

"The great quiet has come," he said.

George nodded and sighed. "I'm as soft as a pussycat," he said. Walling laughed. "Exercise!" he said. "Are you going somewhere this summer?"

"We might. My wife has August off. Maybe we'll go to Vermont. It depends." He felt a somewhat qualified interest in Walling. He had been surprised too that the mathematics teacher sought him out. It was vaguely flattering in the same way that the attention paid to him by the richest boy in his high school had been years ago. Perhaps he attracted loners.

"I'm going to a mathematics encampment in Maine in August," Walling said. "But I don't look forward to it. Lady mathematicians are frightful. They behave like Roman generals. If your fly is open, they're too distinguished to mention it."

"Why don't you come up to see us some Sunday?" George asked. He was suddenly tense. He hadn't meant to ask Walling; he didn't know whether he really wanted him to come.

"That's nice of you. But I won't. I've got myself a show in the fall at the Nestor Gallery—you know it?—and I've got a lot of work to do. But if you're in town . . . drop in to see me. I have a room on Tenth Street where I work. It's crumby."

"I'd like to see your work," George said.

"I don't know about that," said Walling, writing an address down on a scrap of paper, "but we can have a drink."

He turned to go but halted as a girl knocked on the frame of the door. She looked seventeen. She was slender, with drooping shoulders and pulpish thighs, and she was dressed shabbily, almost pitifully, in a rusty blue dress that was too tight across her chest. Her face was clouded with acne, and her lank hair looked wet. She stared desperately at Walling.

"Well, now . . ." he said.

"Could I see you a minute?" she asked.

"You're seeing me."

"Alone?"

"I gather you're distressed about your grade," Walling said. "Don't waste your valuable time. I never change them."

She bit her lower lip histrionically. "You don't even know my name, Mr. Walling," she wailed.

"I know your work," he replied calmly.

She shuddered suddenly, then, her head drooping, turned and ran from the room.

Walling laughed. "I read your face, Mecklin," he said. "You think I was mean to that poor little kid. You're wrong. I'm good for their souls—those minute, shrunken, pale souls lodged somewhere in their gullets. I'm justice without mercy. And you're wrong to waste sympathy on her. In her world, she's a power—the sex queen of the senior class. Even though you may find her unlovely, her favors are fought for. You look a little reedy. Listen . . . take a good look at her in the fall, although by then she may be finished. They have a short term, but while they have it the pretty ones don't have a chance. Ah . . . but in ten years. She'll be a virago with five children, and when their infant hands wander toward their infant loins, she'll knock them out of their high chairs."

"You treat them like enemies," George said.

Walling frowned. "Them? Well, they are." He handed George a box of paper clips from the desk, saluted him with a finger to his forehead and left.

On the way home, George fell into a semisomnolent state. He had been staring at the pale sky drained of color.

Even the landscape looked spent. In a dream that barely took him to the brink of sleep, he saw Walling's sex queen advancing toward him on roller skates. Forked twig, his mind said, you're only a forked twig. As she came closer, he saw her legs gyrate wildly, and the ugly dress slipped from her shoulders, revealing a boy's chest with prominent nipples surrounded by bruised aureoles.

When the train came to a shuddering stop, he awoke into a sweaty seaminess. The plush seats were dark green like moss under water. The car was without sunlight.

He should have been glad; his time would be his own now for nearly three months, but he felt oppressed and breathless. He wondered if he were coming down with something. As he headed the car down Route 129, he realized that what he was suffering from was a profound disaffection with his life.

Perhaps it was only the anticlimax of school closing. Perhaps it would go away when he had rested a few days. He would really *have* that country house now. Yet he wished suddenly he could have gone with Walling. He found his coldness—really, his brutality—repugnant. But the shocks to his own sensibilities which he suffered from Walling's personality gave him a sense of urgency, or perhaps it was energy, which he felt his own life lacked.

Emma, scented with the odor of roast beef, greeted him warmly, and he was surprised and somewhat alarmed. She had made a complicated dinner—the cookbook was still open on the kitchen table when he got home—and had set the table as though company were coming.

She watched him eat as though her fate as a cook hung in the balance. He complimented her, but the food was awful. She had experimented, and there were so many seasonings in everything that they canceled out each other and what remained was the taste of effort. While they were drinking coffee—she had allowed him to make that, and it was strong—she mentioned that Minnie Devlin had dropped by for a visit.

"She isn't so bad, you know," Emma said. "Her stories are marvelous. She has a real comic view. I haven't laughed so much in I don't know how long! She suggested all kinds of ways we could make the living room look bigger. I had a good time with her."

He was listening intently; aware of his attention, she seemed to preen herself. She touched him a good deal on his arms and face. She began sentences and left them unfinished as though to illustrate some childlike spontaneity. They were to be like lovers, like children, like old friends. Then her voice faltered. She eyed the kitchen door as though she had invited someone of whom he would not approve. The atmosphere became feverish. There was a boiling sea of acid in his stomach—he longed for a pill. She dropped a cup and the handle broke. Something obdurate in him sat and waited. She was up to something.

At last, with a deep sigh, delivered from a self-prescribed captivity, she said, "Maybe we ought to go to an analyst."

"That sounds like Minnie's comic view."

"It wasn't only her idea."

"Why?"

"She asked me what happened to the boy you had talked about that night—"

"Wait!" He held up his hand. "You mean you told her about him, is that right?"

"Minnie said . . . Listen, George. Everyone is the child of two parents—"

"Minnie's a storehouse of information, isn't she?"

"We all have weird impulses we don't understand. Do you think you're exempt?"

"What the hell are you talking about?"

"Ernest!" she cried out. "Doesn't it occur to you that your interest in him isn't only educational?"

George sat silent, unmoving, but he felt a kind of interior convulsion as though a part of himself were trying to tear loose from the rest. He was more dismayed than angered; he sat as though bound to his chair by ropes. His captor scraped plates and bound up leftovers in aluminum foil. She spoke harshly but with an odd, nervous humor, as though trying to coax him into an amiable admission of what, after all, was a universal human predilection. Look at cows! Look at the Greeks! Consider Mead's study of certain Fiji tribes. . . .

"Fixation," she said wisely. "Homoerotic," she said jokingly. The dishes rattled in the dishpan. Emma's hands, covered with soap bubbles, gestured, poked the air as if to find the words Minnie had left in her wake.

Still, he sat without speaking. She observed they would have to have the cold water tap fixed—it leaked.

"Say something!"

"Minnie Devlin," he said, "the culture crapper."

She burst into tears. He got up and left her in the kitchen. Then he went upstairs, took two blankets from a chest and threw them on the spare bed. It pleased him not to use sheets. He placed a chair next to the bed, took the alarm clock and the lamp from the table in the bedroom and put them on the chair. He took a carton of unpacked books and shoved it with his foot into the spare room. Then he showered, brushed his teeth, and, stripped down to his underwear, crawled between the blankets. With one hand he began to lift books out from the carton. The third volume was a collection of Elizabethan poetry. He began at the beginning. He felt as he lay there a growing sense of well-being. He heard Emma moving in the other room. She was bumping into things. He was not interested in her. She had fouled herself with another woman's malice. He could understand her resentment against his preoccupation with Ernest—she had never understood it. But now she had given it a name—but it was a name for the division between them. So be it.

He rose early the next morning and took a long walk in the orchard. Although his exhilaration of the night had fallen away, it had left him with a sense of liberation. The orchard swayed in a light breeze; the sky was cloudless and brilliant. He would, from now on, do exactly as he wanted to do.

When he returned, he found Emma making coffee. She looked abject. He asked her if she would like a soft-boiled egg. He intended, he said, to make one for himself. Her mouth turned downward with self-denial. He needn't bother, she said.

He told himself he would be nice to her. She was quite right about an analyst. And the hell with them too. Neither of them spoke of what had happened. But he made his own bed, spreading the blanket so the mattress ticking was entirely covered.

Later, around six in the evening, they had a drink together. The twilight was poetic; the kitchen subaqueous, a cup, a glass touched with a streamer of buttery light. They discussed her vacation. He had thought of Vermont but perhaps she had other ideas? Wherever he wanted to go, she said. Then he would think about it. Suddenly she grasped his hand.

"I've wounded you terribly," she said.

He looked closely at her face. Her hair looked darker than usual, perhaps because the light was waning.

"Lots of people go to psychiatrists," she said.

"Oh yes," he replied. "Why not?"

"I didn't mean you were a fairy. . . ."

"It's very hard to treat. Perhaps I could be adjusted to it."

"I have every reason to know you're not! Don't I?" she cried, smiling uncertainly. Another lie, but how to unearth the truth now?

"Never mind," he said.

"But I feel you're so angry. . . ."

"Not now," he said.

They heard something in the garage. It sounded as though an object were being dragged along the concrete floor.

Ernest pushed open the door. His eyes were blackened. There were bruises all over his face, and blood had clotted and dried in the corner of his mouth. The flesh on the back of his hands was torn.

George went to him and put his arm under his shoulders. As he led him through the living room toward the stairs, he didn't glance at Emma. It was as though he had forgotten she was there.

Chapter Four

A THUNDERSTORM brought in its wake a week of bad weather. Maple branches struck the windows of the Mecklin house; the winds howled through the orchards, where the trees seemed about to rise on end as torrents of rain washed away the mantle of earth and exposed their gray roots. Except where patches of mud had collected, the driveway stood out like a line of chalk on a blackboard. The vegetables in Emma's garden were beaten flat. Even after the rain had thinned and the wind abated, thunder rumbled from the upper reaches of the Hudson Valley.

The electricity failed for a day and a night. George, walking through the living room with a lit candle, saw at a window in the Palladino house another candle on a sill like a watery reflection of his own. The dampness of the roof made maps on the ceilings of the upper rooms. In the spare room where Ernest lay in bed, a pot caught the steady drip of a more serious leak.

Ernest ate everything Emma sent up to him, scraping the plate with an old man's thoroughness. Emma, George observed, was unsettled by those emptied plates. She filled them fuller, and still they came back as though wiped clean. Ernest stayed prone for several days while his bruises turned yellow and thin scabs began to form on his hands. Except when he slept, he chain-smoked the cigarettes George provided. He would not eat when George was in the room; he asked for nothing, only taking what was brought him. When he slept, he looked slight and withered lying so stiffly beneath the blanket. George wondered if he was too bruised to sprawl. Or had he always slept that way?

Up and down stairs George went. The boy watched him silently as he gathered up the overflowing ash tray and the dishes, sometimes stopping to straighten a corner of the blanket. George was surprised every time he entered the room. The boy's presence had brought an element of unpredictability into his life that enlivened the most trivial events of his day. Ernest took what George gave him and he did not thank him. It was an arrangement entirely clear of personal scenery—no smiles of flannel; no phrases trailing off; no display of temperament. It had the simplicity of any expedient relationship. Reluctant to introduce the world of reasons—of cause—George did not ask Ernest what had happened to him. He reminded himself Ernest might have been involved in a crime, in violence, but the thought had no weight. He felt only the fatality of Ernest's presence.

But on a day when Emma was in the city, Ernest told him, and George listened carefully, as though he must prepare an alibi for him.

119

"It was his father," he told Emma that evening. "The radio started it. Ernest took it home. . . . He only wanted it for himself." He glanced at her briefly. She was watching the smoke from her cigarette. "He told his father he'd taken it. . . . The man was drunk. He'd been fired off a construction job out at that colony on the river road. He'd been drinking for two days. He beat him—first with his hands. Then he went after him with a claw hammer."

"He should have gone to the police," said Emma.

"He was afraid—about the radio."

She wanted to say more. He saw it in her face, in the way she shut her mouth tightly as though she were biting off a thread. Instead she told him the car seat was wet. She had left the window open when she parked at the station.

Emma was at home the next day. George worked around the house, and although he had no talent for small repairs, he went about it in an organized fashion, checking them off from a list on a piece of paper he carried around in his shirt pocket.

The tap of his hammer threatened to explode the warm, damp silence of the house as a stone can threaten a landslide. Trying to imagine those upper regions above the dark overcast where the sunlight was, he imagined himself looking down as from a great height; he saw the two houses, little man-made rectangles adrift in a tumult of trees and rain, small points of animal heat imprisoned in squares. Without light, there seemed to be no time. Glancing once at the Palladino house, he saw a window open. A cup was tossed out. It made him laugh—someone was trying to get out.

At some point during that week of Ernest's convalescence, it struck George that all three of them were in hiding; gathering their strength for some purpose still veiled.

It was a revelation to him that his manner had so altered as to produce a look of perplexity on Emma's face; that his thoughts could wander at will, hidden from interpretation. To be reserved—even secretive—satisfied an old longing in him. There was so much about other people he had never understood, not so much the questions of motive or purpose, but the mystery of authority, of substantiality— the way *they* prevented others from *interfering*. Perhaps he was close to discovery; perhaps it was all gimcrack, a cheap cover for his old weaknesses, brought on by a spell of self-righteousness.

With a certain swagger, he had taken to eating between meals, whenever he felt like it. Emma observed. Was she hoping he would relent? Was she looking for vulnerability?

She had submitted to Ernest's presence, speaking to the boy politely, asking him how he felt, cooking for him without complaint. Formality governed their waking hours. Jesus knows, he thought, what we all dream about.

Toward the end of the week Ernest began to sit downstairs in the living room. If Emma had no household work, she kept to the bedroom. The three were rarely together in the same room. When that happened one would always walk away somewhat stiffly like an affronted cat.

On Saturday morning Palladino knocked on the back door. Could he get them anything, he wanted to know? He was going into Peekskill to shop. Martha had flu and was in bed. George looked at him coldly. It was the first time Joe had taken out the car in a week. Unless he'd walked to New York, he and Lila would not have met for all that time.

He wondered how they communicated—perhaps Joe called her late at night, his household asleep. And Lila, sitting in her dusty rooms in the rainy city . . . was she delirious with her habitual dream of abandonment and betrayal?

Under George's scrutiny, Joe nervously lit a bent cigarette. He had clumpy, curved hands like a raccoon's, and the backs of his fingers and hands were covered with fine brown hair. Looking at those hands George had a murky thought of darkness and his sister's fine-grained, slightly damp skin. He shivered, and Palladino apologized for letting in the chill air.

"We don't need anything," George said. Joe's rather narrow eyes examined George's face. Was he looking for a resemblance? For an instant, George perceived what must have charmed Lila—something in Joe's expression that begged for fondness, an ambition to please that was as ingenuous as it was suspect.

"You've been laying my old sister," George said to himself, and smiled at the thought that he might have said it out loud. Joe, apparently taking his smile for a blessing and a dismissal, mentioned the rain pouring through the open doors of the garage and backed away to his car.

Later on George was sitting in the living room, reading to Ernest from *Typhoon*, when a great shaft of pure yellow light flooded through the window and lay upon the floor. They both looked out the windows. The sun floated free in a patch of blue sky.

Suddenly George felt a touch of loneliness which, like a tremor of unexpected pain, evoked in him by its very slightness a knowledge of awful forces yet held in check. The contained, small world the storm had shaped had been broken into; his triumph gave way to a feeling of sadness and loss. His sense of change, after all, had been only a mood of anger. Was true change impossible?

It was not that he had imagined he could long retain his tyranny—there was more, he admitted to himself, of the tyrant in him than he had suspected—but he had hoped for something, self-possession; no, a *little* self-possession. Yet here he was finding it hard to catch his breath, troubled by that familiar sense of obligation to persons known and unknown which had always plagued him like a faint, wearying tic.

"He's good," Ernest spoke suddenly.

George gave him a distracted glance.

"Good? Yes, he's good on storms," he said.

"Maybe I'll read it myself," Ernest said.

"You must be feeling better."

Ernest didn't answer. The sunlight lapped at their shoes.

"It might do you good to take a walk," George said. "The weather is clearing." He sighed involuntarily.

"Yeah," Ernest said.

George left the Conrad anthology on the couch and went upstairs. He opened all the windows. The glare of sunlight on the horizontal white clapboard of the Palladino house hurt his eyes. He squinted, and leaning forward on the sill thrust his head into the bland, washed air. It reminded him that he had to buy screens. During the storm, the house had incubated a community of flies.

"How is he today?"

He turned and saw Emma sitting on the edge of the bed. She was wearing shorts and an old shirt of his.

"He's going to take a walk."

"The mud's a foot thick," she said. "And there's nothing left of the garden . . . a bald spot."

"I'm sorry about that."

"I wouldn't have planted it if I'd known this was going to happen."

It was as though he had not seen her for a long time, and he was surprised she was so much the same.

"You can't get a guarantee . . ." he said.

"I'm glad you told me. . . . You look worried."

He laughed. "Someone once told me that was a Jewish compliment. Or maybe the word was tired."

They heard the kitchen door close. Ernest must have gone out. To control a rising agitation, George told himself he was a bishop; he was walking through a cathedral—Salisbury—and it was late in the evening and he stopped to rest his hand on the cenotaph of a dead knight—

"Are you worried?" she asked.

"I can't remember. . . . When you die in battle do they put the dog at your feet? Or at your head?"

"George!"

He didn't want her to tell him how he looked. He didn't want her tramping around in his head.

"We ought to have the Devlins to dinner," he said.

"The Devlins?" She looked startled.

"We should have done it before now. Why haven't we?"

"I wouldn't have thought you'd care to spend an evening with Minnie," she answered, sounding crisp and crooked.

"You take her seriously," he said. "I don't."

"We'll have to buy liquor."

"We're not so poor."

"What about the Palladinos?"

"No."

She nodded. "I suppose they couldn't come anyhow," she said, "since she has permanent flu."

He wondered at her lack of interest in Lila. It seemed inhuman.

"This business about Lila . . . I'm very concerned."

"What business?"

"With Palladino . . ."

"For God's sake, she's a big girl. . . . Let her run her own life."

"I said I was concerned."

"I doubt if she is." She began to whistle. The high insistent little tune sounded bad-tempered. George walked rapidly out of the room and down to the kitchen. Ernest had gone out. The Conrad volume lay on the kitchen table as though he had first decided to take it with him, then changed his mind. George turned up the flame beneath the coffeepot. Then he heard Emma; a minute later she was standing directly behind him.

"What about the radio? Is he going to bring it back?"

"I haven't asked him to," George said.

"Are you going to?"

"I don't know."

"I want it back."

"A cheap little radio . . . here!" He turned around and shoved his hand in his pocket, taking out some crumpled bills. "Go get another one."

"What are you doing to me?" she asked, her jaws clenched.

"Stop it!" he whispered.

"Stop it? You're killing me!" she cried.

He snorted. "What do you know about being killed? No one's ever raised a hand to you."

"What do you know?"

"Nothing."

"I had a rotten time. . . ."

"You had the childhood of a turnip."

"Why did he steal from you?"

"Why not?"

"You tried to help him. . . ."

He seized her suddenly by the shoulders, feeling her breath on his ear. The money in his hand fell to the floor.

"Don't interfere!" he said.

"It's a mistake . . ." she muttered. "Awful . . ."

"Look! I've showered you with money!"

Around her feet the green bills lay looking shabby and incredibly useless.

"The fact is, he stole," she said weakly, looking down at the floor.

"The fact! Tell me the facts of your life!" He released his grip on her shoulders. She bent down and picked up the money. Although she held it loosely in her hand, he was sure she was counting it. "Or we could settle for the Devlin school of facts. Any day now, I may appear before you wearing rouge and ladies' bloomers."

"I don't know why you're still talking about that," she said miserably. "What did you mean, a *'turnip'* childhood?"

He smiled, because she was closer to him than she had been an hour ago, because he had not really alienated her.

"And what if he's lying to you?" she asked.

"What if he is?" he replied, pitying her because she was only a nervous young woman. How could he expect her to understand what he saw glimmering faintly behind the boy's presence in the house. He hardly understood it himself. I want to do more than endure, he told himself.

It was because Ernest was not a good boy, in Emma's

simple-minded view, that George had been forced up against the walls which, he realized now, had always imprisoned him. What if he couldn't change himself? What if he did have an irksome dependence on the presence of other people? Something had happened.

He embraced Emma and kissed her cheek. "Poor girl," he murmured and felt her stiffen. "I was commiserating with you," he said. She sighed heavily. The disconsolate weight in his arms grew somewhat oppressive.

"The coffeepot handle is burning," he said, and released Emma who began, half-heartedly, to wash dishes.

"I took a walk," said Ernest, appearing suddenly at the door. George wondered if he had been standing in the garage listening to them.

"Good," he said.

"I thought I could do something around the house," Ernest continued, speaking directly to Emma. "To make up for the radio. . . . It's busted. My old man threw it up against the wall. So I could maybe do something, like painting. . . ."

Emma, looking, George observed, thoroughly disconcerted, moved quickly to the stove where she picked up the money she had left on it. She handed the bills to George.

"Ask George," she said, not looking at Ernest, but watching George's hand as he pushed the money back in his pocket.

George smiled to himself. Clever Ernest.

The days lengthened. In the sunny stillness of the orchards, the grass grew high. Cunningham, the landlord, came by one afternoon with his two middle-aged sons. He was an elderly man and he was dressed in a dark blue suit with a vest. As he trudged through his orchards, his sons followed like plainclothesmen. George was hanging a hammock between two maple trees. The old man stopped to speak with him while his sons, in some silent, habitual communication, looked thoughtfully at each other a discreet distance away.

Was everything all right, Cunningham wanted to know? Were they enjoying his little house?

Later, Emma told George she had seen Cunningham speaking to him from the window. He was the same old man who had surprised her so that day in the orchard when they had first moved in. She seemed relieved to discover who he was. Apparently it had been bothering her all along. Some wilted daisies lay on the table. Ernest had picked them, she said, but had neglected to put them in a vase.

"*The* vase, I mean," she said.

"They look past redemption."

"No, no . . . they just need water. I'll put an aspirin in it. That's supposed to revive flowers."

He was amused at the picture of Ernest gathering a bouquet.

"When is Minnie coming?" he asked.

"She said she was driving right over."

The Devlins had been unable to accept Emma's invitation to dinner, although she had offered them a handful of Saturdays to choose from. Weekends were bad, Minnie had explained, because they were Charlie's little creative hours. Week nights were out too because Charlie's work was unpredictable, and often he had to stay in town late. But she had called in the morning to say they were flying to Puerto Rico for a few days. They had a good many perishables she didn't want to throw away and so she would like to bring them over to the Mecklins.

"Where is Ernest?" George asked.

"I think he went down the hill. He dumped the flowers here and took off."

"I want him to be here when Minnie comes," George said. Emma, who was filling the vase with water, turned off the faucet. "Why?" she asked.

"I want her to see him," he said shortly.

He went out the front door of the house onto the gray peeling floor of the small porch and, shading his eyes, looked down the slope. Near the stone wall where Cunningham's property ended, he saw Ernest sitting with his back up against a tree.

He started down the hill toward him. He was probably reading. Although George had tried to involve the boy once more in some makeshift school program, Ernest had refused to take it seriously. He had, he said, "lost" his books, and George had spent an hour in the dusty upper reaches of a textbook outlet store in the city looking for another copy of the history text. He had found it, and, although Ernest sat quietly enough at the kitchen table while George read or talked, there was no response at all. Ernest was often on the edge of sleep.

But he had developed an interest in Conrad. Ever since the morning when George had read him a few pages from *Typhoon*, Ernest had been reading Conrad as though addicted. Everything George could find that had been published in paperback he brought home. Yesterday evening, Ernest had begun *The Heart of Darkness*. George, watching him covertly, wondered what held him so—he noticed that now and then Ernest only read a line before turning the page. What did he skip over, and what did he read with such intensity?

Ernest's eyes were closed as he leaned his head against the tree trunk. The book was held loosely in one hand. The bruises on his face had faded away, and he was no longer pale. There was a faint flush on his cheeks; there were twigs and bits of leaf in his hair as though he had rolled on the ground.

"Hi," Ernest said, his eyes still closed.

"How would you like to paint the porch?"

"I'm crazy to do that thing," said Ernest.

"I thought we'd drive into Peekskill and get paint."

Ernest frowned, opened his eyes and sprang to his feet effortlessly.

"No," he said.

"You'll have to go in sometime. Why not now?"

"Later . . ."

"He's not looking for you. Is that what you're worried about?"

"Him? He's never looking for me."

"Come on, then. . . ."

"I don't want to see *anybody*. I don't want to go in there."

"Well . . . come up to the house anyhow. Let's take a look at the porch."

They began to walk up the hill. As though hurled from slings, grasshoppers shot into the air in front of their moving feet. Ernest caught one in midair.

"Jesus! Look at it!" he said, peering into his curved fist. "It's got a real eye and it's hairy all over. It's green." He flung it at a low-hanging branch of an apple tree.

130

"I've been thinking about something," he said then. "I've been thinking about going to California."

George stood still. They were in front of the house. The drone of insects was like the sound of heat itself, and around their ankles the sword-shaped grass swayed in a ground breeze.

"What for?"

Ernest laughed. "You'll catch flies that way with your mouth open. What do you mean? I can't stay here forever. I know a guy who hitched out there. He got a job. There's a lot of factories. It's warm all the time." He rolled his eyes. "Hollywood, the land of the stars."

"It's three thousand miles from here. What are you going to use for money? Look at your shoes. . . . They'd fall apart before you got to Peekskill."

"You just go," Ernest said quietly.

"It's not so easy."

"One, two, three," Ernest said, marching up to the porch step. "That's how you do it!" He did a soldier's turnabout and stood at attention, his face expressionless.

"What about school?"

Ernest snorted and abruptly sat down on the step.

"Come on! You know that's over. It was over after I learned to read. That's all I need. See . . . I can read the signs. California, twenty-eight hundred miles . . . California, fifteen hundred miles . . . California, one mile . . ."

"You'll be stuck all your life! You haven't any skills. Do you know the kind of jobs you'll have to take? You're not going to be seventeen forever."

"Yesterday I was eighteen."

"You'll end up a bum!" George cried.

"That's how I'm starting."

George didn't want to ask him but he couldn't help himself. "How long have you been thinking about this? All the time you've been here?"

Ernest curved his fist and peered into it over his waggling thumb.

"So you *have* been thinking about it all the time. . . ."

A lock of shaggy black hair slid down Ernest's forehead. "You do this," he said. "Make a fist. Look inside. In there, it's your life. In here, it's mine. You don't see mine inside your hand, do you?"

"I don't want your life. I wanted to help."

"Okay. You helped. But you *asked* me to come here and I came here. We're square." He opened his fist and looked straight at George, his glance traveling over George's face —an impersonal glance, full of disbelief, as though George too were green and hairy. "Mr. Mecklin," he said blandly, "you ought to have a kid. Your wife in there needs shaking up. You know what I mean?" He was laughing silently now—an idiot face.

"You're pretty lousy," George said.

"Yeah . . ."

The front door opened, and Emma and Minnie Devlin stepped out at the same moment, a slender sneaker-shod foot next to a fat ankle stuffed into a pink sling pump.

"Here's Minnie," said Emma needlessly.

"I've brought you a positive feast!" Minnie announced. She was wearing a pink linen dress upon which tiny bits of glass had been sewed, so that as she stepped forward into the sunlight, she flashed and glittered.

They herded into the kitchen like limp sheep and sur-

132

veyed the groceries she had spread out on the kitchen table. An empty straw basket stood under the table's edge.

"She carried it all by herself," said Emma lamely.

"Peasant stock!" Minnie explained loftily. "Nothing like it for carrying burdens!"

George took an inventory of the burdens. There was half an avocado mold, a loaf of *pâté*, a quart of milk, a carton of whipped butter, an open tin of herring fillets, several disintegrating cheeses, the end of a baked ham covered with cherries, chutney, a delicate little porcelain container of French mustard, and a quart jar in which a greenish, murky liquid swarmed with bits of things like an inch of magnified pond water.

"That's homemade soup," Minnie said, pointing to the jar. "Charlie likes good food, but—can you imagine?— it's Trevor who goes for the *pâté*. I don't know *who* he gets his exotic tastes from. Charlie and I are quite simple in our tastes. Now . . . when we get to Puerto Rico, Charlie will find the real authentic restaurants where you can get the true food of the people. That's what we want!"

As she spoke, Minnie looked rapidly from Emma to George as though, George thought, she was trying to gauge the exact effect of her words so that later she could come to some conclusion about herself. Ernest, slouched against the living-room doorway, suddenly sniggered. Minnie turned with sinister rapidity as if to put herself within striking range. Ernest stared at her fixedly.

"Of course, you must be Ernest. Yes. I've heard about you."

Ernest said nothing. George felt as if his own personal army had just fixed bayonets.

"Ernest?" inquired Minnie of the ceiling. "Ernest . . . ?"

"Ernest Kurtz," answered Ernest, smiling at George.

"Kurtz? German?"

"Belgian," said George quickly. He wanted to laugh. He wanted to take Ernest by the arm and leave that kitchen to the two women, Emma and her doggy gratitude for some-one else's leavings, and Minnie, the peasant queen, in her glass dress.

"I understand Mr. Mecklin is helping you with your schoolwork."

"That's what he does," said Ernest.

"Well . . . you're very lucky, aren't you?"

"That's right. I'm lucky," replied Ernest.

"You said this was a business trip, Minnie," Emma cut in nervously. "Something to do with the program?" Minnie backed a few steps, keeping Ernest in view.

"Yes. Well, there are some very positive things going on in Puerto Rico. Charlie is going to collect some fairly important educators, artists—he's very interested in the creative process—and fly them up here for interviews. A kind of little series in a big series . . . you know . . . Puerto Rican renaissance."

She clasped her hands around the handle of her purse.

"Oh!" she exclaimed. "You should have seen the response we got to that delinquency series! Thousands of letters! You don't have a set, do you? Charlie is guesting on a panel next week. Too bad . . . but you could *listen* to the radio program. It's all so sensitively done. Charlie has such *feeling* for underprivilege." She stared grossly at Ernest. He lit a cigarette, keeping his eyes on her.

134

When she is silent, she is very silent, George thought, and found himself interested in her. She vomits speech, then retreats, like some mud dweller. Did she decide to become the person she was, he wondered? He was suddenly convinced that Minnie detested everyone, starting with old Charlie.

"Well, enjoy your goodies," she said at that moment. "I've *got* to go. We're leaving in the morning, and I've a million things to do. Is Martha in, would you know? I thought I'd drop by a minute to see how the poor thing is doing. Speaking of deterioration . . ." She giggled. "Not that we were. . . . I don't know what I was thinking about . . . but you know all about it, I'm sure." She looked enigmatically at George—or so she imagined, he thought. "He's charming, isn't he?" she asked. "Joe. Absolute death on women!"

After she left, Emma ran to the living room.

"She's stopping in front of the Palladinos," she called out. "She's getting out of the car. She's walking toward the back door. She's kicking one of the children's toys out of her path. My God! Now she's coming back. She's poking her hair. She's getting in—unh! Hard to be plump! She's driving off!"

George saw the baby-blue car slide out of view. Emma laughed maliciously. "I bet she got thrown out!" She hitched up one shoulder. He had never seen her do that before. But if he had only just noticed it, why did he find it so hateful, he wondered?

"It's what you might have done to her once," he said so bitterly that he choked, and coughing out the other things he might have said, turned his back on her reproachful face.

"That's a bundle of joy," said Ernest.

"Let's have coffee and eat Trevor's *pâté*," George said.

Ernest's appetite had abated somewhat in the last few days, and he picked at the food without interest. He frequently looked out the window, then bent forward and hunched over his shoulders, his hands clasped beneath the table. The *pâté* had a faintly spoiled taste like leftover party food. Emma sighed as she ate the inside of several pieces of bread, piling the crusts on the table.

He would be gone, George thought. He would be a speck in the vast interior reaches of the country. It was a rotten idea. What kind of work could he get? California was a bad state for unskilled labor.

He sickened at the food—a pervasive sense of loss filled the dinky, unkempt little room. What were they all doing there? When would Ernest leave? But he couldn't ask. He couldn't stop him. There was nothing he could do at all.

"I'll paint the porch first," Ernest said, as though he had heard George's thoughts. It was funny of him to pick Kurtz from all the Conrad names he might have taken. But then, it was the right one for Minnie. Mrs. Would-Be Dr. Schweitzer meets Mr. Kurtz. . . .

George went off to Peekskill to get the paint. While he was gone Lila telephoned. Emma said she had sounded agitated. Ernest was opening the deck paint and peering into the can with a child's interest in thick liquids.

"She wants you to call right away."

"She can wait," George replied irritably. "Ernest, get out of that paint can! It's too late to start today."

"I can do that porch in an hour."

"Not if you're going to do a decent job."

"I'll do it right. It's not the first time I've painted."

George picked up the flat top and wedged it back on the container. "Not today!" he said emphatically. Ernest shrugged, then followed him out to the porch where George stamped his feet on the loose boards. "Anyhow, it has to be hosed down and scraped," he said.

The porch sloped perceptibly. Rambler roses straggled untidily over the steps. The whole house needed painting; the roof leaked; a line of tiles had come loose from the bathroom wall. Furthermore, the car sounded as though it were about to break out with muffler trouble. One foot on the bottom step, one foot on the hummocky ground, George looked at the house. In the fields the insects sounded like metal filings in a wind tunnel. His sense of harassment intensified. He should have complained to Cunningham instead of grinning and nodding over the old man's pleasantries. He noticed that Emma was watching him through the window. On top of everything else, he was being spied on. He scowled, and she disappeared. Where she had stood, he saw the big chair and the staircase. The house was too small for their habits. Nothing could look more disordered and sleazy than a small house furnished with ratty furniture. Where in hell did the money go?

"What is your name, Ernest. I want it now. You'll tell me, or I'll beat it out of you!" He thought he had shouted, but the boy was leaning forward as though he couldn't hear him. "Your name . . ." he said.

"Jenkins."

George began to laugh. He flopped to the step, bent over and laughed into his hands. "Jesus . . ." he muttered. "What did I think it would be?" He glanced up to where the boy was standing. He looked sullen, resentful. "That's it?" he asked.

"For crissakes . . ." Ernest said and went into the house.

It had been better when Ernest was only Ernest. He stood up and took a few slovenly steps into the grass. The trouble is, one never thinks one is going to get any older. It wasn't that as a young man he had had no intimations of disaster. What had been unimaginable was the indignity of balancing on the edge of shabbiness. He shouldn't have sold the furniture in the Yonkers house. It had seemed so massive then, so ugly and useless. And he and Lila had needed every penny they could get hold of.

He had sold the house to a Yonkers contractor. With the money, they had paid off the nursing home where Mrs. Mecklin had spent the last blind months of her life, and then they had bought a piece of cemetery ground near White Plains into which their mother's coffin had been lowered, swaying slightly as it went. Into the ground with them!

He had gone off to Europe for a year, and Lila and her fish-faced husband had moved into an apartment in Greenwich Village. His share had lasted to the day when he had collected his master's degree from Columbia. It had been hard—like crawling through a tunnel meant for a man half his size—but he had made the money last. He had been thin then. He supposed Lila had fancied herself an heiress until the last nickel was spent.

The house was still standing, although a small housing project had been built around it. George had seen the house in the early spring when, tired of the parkway, he had driven up Warburton Avenue on his way home. The front door was hanging from one hinge. Most of the veranda had been bricked up. He had not stopped to look through the broken windows.

138

He supposed he had better call Lila, though he was in no mood for her self-generated turmoil. She answered instantly, as though she had been sitting by the phone. Would he come to New York? Right away?

"I can't now," he said. "What's the matter?"

"I can't possibly go into it over the phone. I wouldn't ask if it weren't important," she said. Had anything that concerned her ever been unimportant?

"Why don't you and Claude come out here," he asked, wondering if he could stand them all in the house. What if it rained?

"That's out! My God! How do you think I'd feel with *her* next door?"

"I suppose it's something about that?"

She didn't answer at once, but her ragged breathing crept into his ear like a worm.

"That!" she said bitterly. "Yes. What else would you call it?"

"I'll come in tomorrow."

"When?"

"I don't know. Around noon probably."

"George . . . thank you. You *are* good to me. I know it's hard."

"Do you still have your job?"

She laughed richly. "Of course! I wouldn't call you this way if it were just a matter of that!"

He smiled grimly into the receiver. Of course you wouldn't, he thought. What is employment compared to true love?

He barely spoke to Ernest the rest of the day. After a silent supper, he insisted brusquely that Emma go to the movies with him. They sat through half of a musical comedy whose penny-candy colors barely concealed the advancing decrepitude of its actors. An extraordinarily loud kiss echoed in the black upper reaches of the balcony. George turned indignantly as a hard, female giggle erupted in the back rows.

"Let's go," he said.

"It might get better."

"It'll never be as good," he said.

They stumbled over knees and feet, up the aisle and out into the silent street. It felt early. The thought of returning home oppressed him. He stood irresolutely beneath the movie marquee while Emma waited, looking down at her shoes.

"Let's go for a drive," he said. She nodded without looking up.

They drove north out of Peekskill. On their left the dark river glinted where moonlight touched it. When they came to the Bear Mountain Bridge, George drove off the road onto a parking area girdled with chunks of granite. The bridge, looking fragile for all its bulk, was lit with amber lights. The east and west side of the valley were so close at this point that the bare rock of the hills seemed to have been cleaved by a single ax blow.

"It looks like a bridge for a toy train set, doesn't it?" said Emma. "As if you could pick it up and reassemble it."

"I suppose. . . ."

"Did you have trains when you were a kid?"

"No."

"Didn't you want them?"

"I never thought about it," he said, wondering if he ever had.

"I was always thinking about what I didn't have. When

my aunt sent my mother a check for my Christmas present, she always used it for my clothes. It was unfair."

"What would you have spent it on?"

"Oh, God . . . the list is so long."

"You still have a list?"

"I've always had one. I add to it all the time. It's gotten so long now I can't remember what it starts out with. How were your Christmases?"

"Poor."

"It was the only time of year we went to church."

He laughed. "When Lila was twelve she developed a sudden interest in God. She joined a Dutch Reformed church for a year. It drove Mama wild. She suspected Lila was praying against her. Not that she believed in higher powers. It's strange . . . what happened to her. You know, she was a feminist. But she narrowed so as she got old. Maybe it was my father's dying. She had always thought illness was a moral failing—until she got sick herself."

"She didn't like Lila?"

He hesitated, trying to remember, trying to unearth the buried landscape of his childhood.

"It wasn't that," he said. "I don't think it had to do with liking. She was more interested in Lila than she was in me. 'Go see what she's doing,' she'd ask me. I'd run upstairs. Lila wouldn't be in her room. Then I'd go up to the attic. There she'd be, sitting on an old pile of *National Geographics*, staring off into space. When she bothered to notice me, she'd smile and ask, 'Did Mama send you?' and I'd say 'Yes,' and Lila would laugh."

"But you did have some good times, didn't you?"

"Oh . . . yes. That year in Europe made up for a good deal."

"And you didn't mind the army."

"I didn't like Texas."

"You had that girl there. What was her name? Something peculiar."

"Dina."

"Dina. From what you told me, you certainly had a good time with her."

He turned the ignition on.

"I mean," Emma said, "love-making in the woods . . ."

"There weren't any woods where I was. It was as flat as a butcher's board."

"In the tall grass then."

He turned to look behind him as he backed the car onto the road. Emma was sitting forward, her hands gripped in her lap.

"That was a long time ago," he said.

"But you really liked her, didn't you? Even though she was fat. You said she was kind of fat and wore ankle socks."

"It was finding out . . . that first excitement. That's all."

"Don't shout at me!"

"I wasn't shouting." He started down the road toward home. "Didn't you ever have that?" he asked. "Didn't you—"

"Nothing," she interrupted. "No. I didn't."

"In college . . ."

"Not in college. Nowhere."

"Emma . . ."

Later on he said, "It was nice. I was wishing we could go on driving. I don't know where. Far away."

"And leave Ernest behind?" she asked.

"You're going to feel bad pretty soon," he said.

"Just excitement . . ." she muttered.

Dina, so often invoked over the years as to become their chief ghost, humbly trotted around the side of the abandoned fruit-packing plant a few miles from Houston where they had once met. He could see her clearly: she was wearing ankle socks and saddle shoes, and a shapeless cotton dress printed with faded poppies. She had been fat, he supposed, but not repellently as Emma had made it sound. She had smelled of laundered cotton, of soap, faintly of vinegar and strongly of a certain talcum—Mavis, he had discovered. Sometimes she had brought him things to eat: radishes, hard-boiled eggs, Nabisco crackers stuck together with dried peanut butter. In the late afternoons, birds came to drink from a stock pond a few yards away where two cottonwood trees grew.

Excitement. Her innocence, but not his; he had been ashamed to take her where they could be seen together by the soldiers from his barracks—his rough country girl. In that empty landscape where only the two trees and the toppling uprights of the shed gave shelter, they had stumbled toward each other, falling into the prickly dust in a thick, graceless embrace, their faces straining against each other's shoulders like two swimmers racing desperately for opposite shores. What did Emma imagine it had been like?

He could have told her of the desultory aftermath, of his return to the camp, of his uncalled-for lies to which no one listened anyway.

He could have reassured her at the cost of his pride, if he turned Dina over, as it were, to Emma to pick apart. Besides, he had inadvertently liked her. Remembering his shame of her, he was ashamed again for his cowardice, and when Emma asked him later in synthetic concern about Lila, he answered her with a harshness that was really directed toward himself.

He took an early train in the morning—he had wakened with an urgent desire to get out of the house—and from Grand Central took a bus to the West Side where he went directly to the bus terminal. A one-way ticket to Los Angeles cost eighty-four dollars. It was good for sixty days, the clerk said, and George felt he had been given a sentence for an unspecified offense. The clerk's sexless hands moved toward tickets; George shook his head. "Not now . . ."

Thinking of how he could conceal from Emma the withdrawal of such a large amount of money from his checking account—she seemed to know approximately what he had —he walked up Eighth Avenue feeling the sweat form under his jacket in the special midtown heat of the city. It was too early to go to Lila's. Columbus Circle was a few blocks ahead. He decided suddenly to go to the Central Park Zoo. He had not been there for years, and the idea of having something cool to drink at the zoo cafeteria held an unexpected charm.

He walked all the way, heavy with the knowledge of Ernest's ultimate departure, a dark backdrop against which his thoughts played like ineffectual points of light.

At an iron table surmounted by a striped umbrella, he drank a glass of orange juice and surveyed the half-empty zoo arcades. Nearby an elderly man read a newspaper aloud to himself in a toneless mumble.

In the lion house the big cats lay on planks, their dappled bellies rising and subsiding as they slept in the

144

dank, hot air. Only an ocelot stalked the length of its cage, eyes glassy and unfocused as it paced, while harsh mewlings issued from its yellow throat. The seals drew circles through air and water, while above the pool on a projecting cement apron a bull seal sobbed through its sunlit snout.

The monkey house was almost empty. It looked very small, and as gray as official waiting rooms where immigrants sit with numbered cards hanging from their necks. Except for a chimpanzee who rolled around its own hairy arm, wrist bent flat on the stone floor, the monkeys seemed distressed and lethargic. They had nothing to do. George was struck by their boredom, more human than their features. Several small Spanish-speaking children were laughing at a baboon who, having defecated, was examining its feces as though through a jeweler's glass. Better than doing nothing, George thought.

He bought a bag of peanuts from a vendor and gave them one by one to the tattered, obsequious pigeons. Then he threw the bag into a trash basket, aware that he had used up some time he had allotted himself, and that if he lingered any longer among the animals he would not get to Lila's that day.

When he arrived at her apartment, he found the door unlocked and behind it in the dimly lit room Lila sitting in a straight chair, her hands crossed on a book in her lap, an expression of gravity and languor on her face. It occurred to him that she might be pregnant and, appalled, he glanced at her belly, concealed by the blue folds of a bathrobe. Her straggling hair, a general air of disarray, her bare feet protruding beneath the terry cloth seemed to him critical omens of disintegration.

"Where's Claude?" he asked nervously.

"A friend took him to the beach," she said. "Harriet Krebs . . . a friend from the old days . . . nobody you know."

Of course she must have friends. A society of sobbing ladies? Rough, aging girls?

"Have you read this recently?" she asked, holding up a copy of *The Red and the Black*. "I've been rereading it." Holding the book in both hands, she looked at it broodingly. "He knew about women," she said and sighed and let the book drop back in her lap. An old impatience stirred in him; why couldn't she be direct? Why was she so elaborate?

"Listen, George . . ." she began. "This is what happened. Joe and I were having a sandwich and a drink in that bar and grill near the bookstore. Who do you suppose walked in?"

"Stendhal?"

"Minnie Devlin with a gaggle of girl friends. Of course . . . she spotted us instantly. She stumped over to our booth and threw her arms around Joe and kissed him. Where had he been keeping himself, and how was Martha, and how were the children, and was he working, and she and Charlie had been *dying* to see them and—"

"Is that what's worrying you? Because if that's it—"

"Wait," she cried. "She didn't even speak to me! Can you imagine it? She just gave me a look—an arrow through the heart . . . yes . . . that's how she looked at me."

"Minnie wouldn't be caught dead with an arrow. It might give Trevor ideas," he said. He was still standing in front of her. She groaned and threw up her hands. She hadn't asked him to sit down. She was either oblivious to anything but the enactment of her own drama or else was excessively polite. The poor little match girl, or the lady of the manor. He sat down on the corner of a studio bed, then, aware of how dark the room was, got up and went to the window to pull up the blinds.

"No!" cried Lila. "Not yet!"

"It's like night in here."

"Please!"

He let the blinds fall.

"What do you care about Minnie?" he asked. "She's too illiterate to be anything but personal and interfering."

"What does illiteracy have to do with it?"

"I mean . . . she doesn't *know* anything at all. How can you care about her judgment?"

"It's not her judgment I'm worried about."

"It's not like night, it's like a bar. . . ."

"Oh George! Listen . . . She called Martha that afternoon and told her she'd seen us together. When Joe got home that night, Martha was lying on the kitchen floor with her head in a serving platter. She was so drunk she couldn't stand up. Those miserable children!"

That, thought George, was why Minnie had stopped by to see Martha yesterday, to consolidate her gains.

"There's no reason why you can't have a drink with a man," George said.

"I'm only thinking of Joe," Lila insisted. But he knew she wasn't.

When they were still children she had locked him in her room once, and he, excited by the sight of the long, flat key in her hand—there had been a token struggle but he hadn't really wanted to unlock the door—had listened as she told him in fierce whispers of plots against her, of

147

girls who laughed at her clothes, who watched everything
she did, even in the bathroom, because they were jealous.
Jealous of what? he had asked. A curious smile, a vague
gesture of her hands. Oh . . . certain things. Then, her
breath warm on his face, she told him she couldn't stand it.
She couldn't bear everyone watching her, thinking about
her!

As he grew older and more detached, he observed that
much as Lila shrank from attention she also invited it.
As a young girl she had dressed flamboyantly, and there
had been then as there still was a knowing smile on her
face, a smile that made people look quickly over their
shoulders. What was she smiling at? Who?

There had been a girl he had loved all through high
school, a strong blond with fine, white teeth and a kind of
noble amiability that had reminded George of horses. He
had been too timid to ask her out. But once in his freshman
year, the same one in which Lila graduated from the
Yonkers high school, the blond girl asked him if Lila
was his sister, and when he had answered, she had shaken
her large, handsome head at him. "Freakish," she had
said in a kindly way. He had not pursued the conversation.
It wouldn't have mattered what else she might have said.
He already knew.

Remembering now—the long key, the locked door—he
looked at Lila impatiently.

"You always did care too much about what people
thought of you," he said.

She looked at him reflectively.

"You know what, George? You don't have any expression on your face. Mama used to say you were like a
pumpkin waiting to have a face carved on it. Oh . . . you

frown, sometimes you laugh, but even when you're angry, everything stays in place. No clues. What *are* you thinking about?"

"I'm wondering if you asked me to come into the city just to tell me Minnie saw you," he said calmly, while a voice cried out in him silently—betrayed! The two of them, Mama and Lila hiding out somewhere in the ramshackle house behind a closed door, talking about him. She laughed suddenly.

"I see something," she said mysteriously.

George stood up, his breathing was shallow. The airless room had a smell of stagnation, of boiled tea, of powder and stale hairbrushes, of women, he thought.

"Where are you going?"

"That's a hell of a reason to drag me down here," he said.

"Wait! Please . . . it isn't all. Of course, it isn't. I'm in trouble. Awful trouble. The thing isn't good."

"What 'thing'?" he asked sardonically.

"Joe and me. It's a thing, all right." She was suddenly overcome; she buried her face in her hands and rocked back and forth. "He can live without me," she murmured. "He can live without anything except that insane marriage!" She stared up at George. How ravaged she looked!

"I've been ransacked," she said, "not loved. I don't care about anything else anymore. And it's the first time I've ever felt—"

"Oh Christ! The first time! That's what we always say. There isn't any first time."

"You don't know," she moaned.

She stood up and, perversely, he sat down.

"Anybody can have him!" she cried. "He's monstrously

vain! God—I don't even like to sleep with him. He's a lump . . . a lump! Do you know what his idea of intimacy is? It's to pee with the bathroom door open! I'm crazy! What do I want with a man like that? You may well ask . . ." she gurgled. "I should say. And listen, he can't stand me! I revolt him. But, see . . . he's too vain. He can't let go. How do you like that, pally? Disgusting, isn't it? And what comes next? Shall I devote myself to Claude?" She swayed slightly, then bent forward and said in a conspiratorial voice: "Listen, George. Claude's nuts!"

Helplessly, George began to laugh. Lila lifted her hands as though to strike him. But her grimace of rage trembled, broke. Her lips widened and suddenly she was laughing. Standing over him, she bent forward clutching her ribs. George fell back against the wall—as she straightened up again, he leaned forward over a convulsion of laughter that exploded upward. "No more . . ." he gasped, and she shrieked, collapsing onto the straight chair, leaning sideways, a rag doll, heaving, breathless. They were falling apart—their arms hung limply from marshmallow sockets, their ribs ached, tears ran down their faces.

"Oh, what happened?" she squeaked. They were off again, drowning, flailing the dead air with their arms. Slowly, they subsided. Then they were silent; ghostly smiles played about their mouths. For an instant, George wondered if this was how Lila and Mama had laughed about *him*?

"Well . . ." he began. She giggled faintly. "It doesn't look so good."

"What made you laugh?" she asked.

"I don't know," he replied truthfully.

"I suppose it *is* funny in an awful way. . . ."

"No, no . . . that isn't it."

She grinned. It was hard to believe she was forty. She was always Lila, a few years older than he—those were the only years that counted, those few.

"Why don't you stop seeing him?" he asked.

She made a sound of exasperation. "I can't."

"What did Martha say when Minnie called her?" he asked curiously.

"Nothing. She never says anything. When she's drunk, she laughs at him. When she's sober, she's silent."

"That's not what I heard," he said.

"What?"

"Nothing. Gossip."

"I'd like to know."

He shook his head. "After all," he said, "having a drink with him . . ."

"That kind of man? There isn't anything in his life but seduction."

"Lila, don't tell me about him. Listen. I want to say something about Claude."

"The first time we made love . . ." She looked at him quickly. He turned his head away. "The first time, he said he was glad he wasn't a homosexual. What kind of a thing is that? I think women repel him. I think, each time, he feels a little safer—so it always has to be different—"

"Don't! You sound like Minnie."

"You have to admit things aren't what they look like."

"Maybe they are. Exactly." Then he asked abruptly, "Why don't you take Claude to an analyst? There's something wrong there."

"That's what his father says. Only his father says it's me," she answered morosely. "It's awfully expensive, you know."

"What about clinics?"

"Philip would count it as a victory."

"And that's what counts with you?"

"I'll stop seeing Joe," she said in a flat voice. "The next time he comes here, I won't answer the door." She laughed fruitily. "Then the next time, if he comes again, I'll throw my arms around him and press and press and press!"

George got up to go. He made a show of looking at his watch but he didn't care what time it was.

"Won't you have some coffee? A drink?"

"No. I've got to get back."

"I'm sorry," she said. "I needed to talk to someone. You, I guess."

"There isn't anything I can tell you, is there? Not really." He was impatient now to escape the dark room. He didn't even want to look at her in her raveling bathrobe.

She looked at him sadly. "Well, it was nice to laugh," she said.

"Yes," he said. "That was nice."

He went to a movie after he left her. It was a first-run house, and he felt a touch of guilt as he handed two dollars to the ticket seller. The theater was nearly empty. As he walked down the aisle, a subtitle was imposed on the screen. He read the words, "I can't leave you," and heard their Italian counterpart. A man's naked shoulders covered most of the screen. When George sat down, the man had shifted, and around his shoulder appeared the handsome, languid face of a young woman, also naked. More of it, he thought.

Didn't anybody think about anything else? He watched the suggestive coiling and uncoiling and wondered what he was supposed to be looking at. Were they or weren't they? No—just talking. The camera must have slid beneath the bed while the other thing was going on. What were the other people in the audience thinking about? Why did one watch other people? He had seen a pornographic movie once in England and, feeling diminished and swinish, watched with growing terror as the new upstairs maid was had in rapid succession by the lord, the lady and the sons of the manor house. Porno . . . the dominant influence of harlots.

Emma had wanted to know about Dina, about *it*. Had he secretly tried to imagine Joe and his sister in a lyrical embrace? All splendid shoulders and shadowed eyes and mouths? What about the root connection hidden there beneath the sheets? What about that?

The young hero in the movie shot himself ultimately. He had nothing to live for—his friends offered him heroin, religion, domesticity. He could get food and sex for himself. It wasn't enough. Life was a bore.

He had paid two dollars for this, George reflected, and all he could think about was Joe Palladino with the bathroom door open while Lila, adrift in her long, thick hair, listened bitterly from the studio bed.

By the time George got home, he had determined to buy Ernest the bus ticket for California. He would draw a check for cash, and if Emma inquired directly, he would say he was loaning it to Walling. She wouldn't care about Ernest once he was out of the house.

The ticket would be his last gift to Ernest, perhaps the only one from Ernest's viewpoint. George had done what he could. Did it matter if the boy didn't know the Middle Kingdom from his elbow? He had gotten a sense of possibilities, hadn't he? Hadn't they both? He knew George liked him; it was unlikely anyone had before—or even looked at him.

Emma was looking shifty, he thought. She avoided his eyes and busied herself extravagantly with some sewing.

"It wasn't worth the trip," he said. "Minnie ran into Lila and Joe in some bar. Lila seems to think it was important. Minnie told Martha."

"Maybe it is important."

"Why?"

"You can't tell about people like Martha."

Her voice irritated him; it was portentous.

"What does that mean?"

"How do I know? She might shoot him."

"Who might shoot who?"

"People behave irrationally. Maybe you didn't know that."

"What's the matter with you?"

"What do you really want, George?"

He groaned inwardly. It was a question dictated by exasperation; it meant, whatever you want it is inferior and meaningless. "A drink," he said.

"You haven't asked about Ernest."

"Asked what?"

"He's sulking in the orchard. He's out there because I threw a plate at him." She paused. When he said nothing, she went on. "I could have called the police. He made a pass at me." Her voice rose sharply, as though she had stuck herself with the needle. "What do you think of that?"

"Now you're starting up!" he shouted.

She jumped to her feet, dropping a spool of thread to the floor. "My God! Is that all you can say?"

154

It was all he had been able to say; he held his head in his hands, bewildered because he had felt only exasperation.

"What did he do?" he asked at last, looking at her. Her face was swollen, as though her feelings were inflating her. He didn't know what to do with her or with himself.

"He knocked into me . . . in a certain way. I was coming downstairs and he was coming upstairs and right there in the middle of those damned stairs, he shoved himself up against me. I pretended it was an accident . . . for a few minutes. But when I was in the kitchen, I knew how it had really been. He pushed me on the breast. Then I got a plate and went up again. He was lying on the bed reading and when I came in, he smiled. I threw the plate at him. It missed. It just rolled off the bed and broke."

"That's all?"

"Any man but you would have been out the door by now. Anyone but you would have gone after him."

"Look," he said, taking a step toward her. She moved back instantly. "You could be mistaken. Kids get abstracted. They don't move gracefully."

She laughed harshly. "Ernest is graceful. Ernest is a goddamned sylph."

"He wouldn't do it," he said stubbornly.

"He made a pass at me."

"I'd hardly call it that."

"Call it what you like. He put his hand on me."

He looked at her blouse. Barely perceptible were the shapes of her small breasts. She covered them with her hands.

"I'll take him away now. He's going anyway. He told me so yesterday."

"Are you going to say anything about this?"

"I'll say something."

"Don't you care?"

"Yes . . . I care." Then he stopped; he was too tired.

He got a paper bag from the kitchen and collected a few books for Ernest. There wasn't anything else except the toothbrush and razor he'd bought him, a handful of ragged clothes. Emma followed him, watching. Did she think he was going to steal something? He turned on her angrily once, and she started back away from him. One large luminous tear was on her cheek; dazzled by its brilliance, he watched it run under her chin and disappear. Perhaps, he thought, he was crazy. The weight . . . the weight of everything was stupefying.

He went out to the car. Ernest was standing there in the garage. "Let's go," George said.

Ernest got into the car without a word. Neither spoke until George turned onto the highway. Then Ernest asked where they were going.

"I'm taking you to Peekskill. Tomorrow I'm going to buy you a bus ticket for Los Angeles. I can give you fifty dollars along with the ticket. It'll help see you through until you get a job."

"I'm not going to Los Angeles."

George hardly heard. "What happened there on the stairs?" he asked.

"She threw a plate at me."

"Why?"

"I ran into her. I was thinking about something. I didn't even see her. Then she comes up a minute later and throws that plate."

It was so much as George had wanted it that he instantly doubted Ernest was telling the truth. He felt nothing at that moment except a vast suspicion of Emma, Ernest, himself, of everyone. Had he only awakened now from the long sleep which his life had been to discover that he could trust nothing?

"Is that all? Did you touch her?"

Ernest was silent. In that silence, George knew, the truth was contained. Would it matter what Ernest said now?

Then Ernest said, "Yeah. I pushed her away. I thought she was going to fall down on me."

"And that's all?" George asked again.

"You're sore too?"

"I'm sick of you!" George said.

"I don't want your lousy ticket."

"The bank is closed now. I'll drive in tomorrow morning. You'd better take care of things. I suppose you ought to tell your father where you're going. I'll pick up the ticket tomorrow afternoon, then I'll meet you somewhere in the late afternoon."

"Didn't you hear me? I don't want that ticket."

"Have you changed your mind about going?"

"I'm going the way I'm going." Ernest hesitated. "Give me the money," he said. "I'll get the ticket myself."

"Cut it out! I won't do that. You might decide to blow the money on something else. If you're serious about this, I'll help you. My way."

"I'll turn in the ticket for the money. . . . What for? What are you doing this for?"

"To show my confidence in you." Hearing his own words, George was struck by their palpable insincerity. His words . . . They were all out in front, and he was lying behind them. "You won't take the trouble to exchange the ticket," he said coldly.

"Show me?" asked Ernest softly.

"I want to do something for you." That was true, wasn't it, George asked himself.

"You can give me five bucks so I can replace that hat you wrecked. And you can drop me in front of the movie."

Ernest was smiling; his hand was on the door handle.

"You wrecked the radio, I wrecked the hat. We'll call it square," George said. He paused, watching Ernest's fingers tighten on the handle. "I'll meet you at ten in front of the bank," he said. "And you can do what you want with the money." Ernest seemed about to say something. Then he was out the door. He leaned on the window. Someone behind George honked his horn.

"Good-bye, Mr. Mecklin." Ernest stepped up the curb and walked rapidly away down the street.

The long twilight was nearly over when George got home. No lights had been turned on. Emma was sitting in the living room.

"He's gone," George said. "It's over. You don't have to put up with him any more."

He turned on a lamp. "Do you want a drink?" he asked.

She shook her head.

He poured some whiskey into a small glass.

"He told me what happened," he said. "It sounded to me as though he didn't have any idea of what you were angry about."

She laughed.

"Now it's funny?"

"You were gone all day," was all she said. He felt a faint ripple of terror like a cat's paw moving across the surface of his mind.

"What about it?"

"After the plate broke, he said we'd better pick up the

pieces. It was so quiet here. The country *is* quiet. There aren't any shades in the spare room. The sun was bright—I could *see* everything so clearly."

"What are you talking about?" he asked, his voice climbing up weakly from a great depth.

"You forced me!" she said savagely. "It was so quick. I didn't know it could be so quick. Why . . . it isn't anything at all, is it? He said you were a dumb son of a bitch. He said you were a creeping Jesus."

He leaped at her; his hands went around her throat. They struggled violently, then she hit him in the stomach and his hands dropped away. They stood facing each other.

"You made it up. You want an excuse. You're jealous of him!" his voice rose in a triumphant cry.

"You dumb son of a bitch!" she said. She was crying now, but her voice was stony.

She slipped past him and went upstairs. He heard her opening drawers. He heard the snap of a suitcase closing. Then she came downstairs, her hair neatly pulled back, carrying a suitcase. She stopped by the table and picked up the stone fetish, slipping it into her handbag. Without a glance at him she phoned a Peekskill cab company. He heard the back door close. The silence heaved itself up at him.

A while later, a taxi drove up the driveway. He listened to the slam of the door, the receding sound of the motor as it went down to the road.

He drank the rest of the whiskey, sitting in his chair, waiting like someone in the basement of a shattered house for the last rafter to fall.

Chapter Five

*T*HE DARK fell. Inside the room the simple shapes of chairs and tables, stairs and window sills were swallowed up, erased. George couldn't hear his own breathing. This is what it is like, he thought, when a tree falls in the forest and no one is there.

His concrete self, the terminal of a web of incident from which it had been severed, sat there, a sack of guts. If it had not been for a thin pain in his bladder, he might, he thought as he went up the stairs, have stayed there until morning.

The shadowless porcelain of the bathroom fixtures, anonymous as stones, could have been anywhere. The toilet flush went through its subsiding convulsion. Through the window he saw a cartoon moon neither near nor far.

The kitchen smelled of tea and stale yellow cheese. He opened a can of sardines and ate them with his fingers, the oil sliding down his chin and onto his shirt, then drank from the whiskey bottle, leaving it uncapped on the counter.

Without thought—a sense that the house had no power to hold him—he walked out to his car. Had Emma looked back? He supposed not. Anger made her draw her head into her shoulders, her arms to her sides, as though she were strung on one cord. Head down, suitcase knocking against her knees, she must have thrust herself into the taxi, looking at nothing, giving directions to the driver in a voice that said he too was part of the world's conspiracy.

Where, he wondered, would she stay tonight? With friends? She had spoken now and then about the women she worked with in the library; one was involved in an interminable divorce litigation, one had cancer, most of them were unmarried. Emma hated hotels—she suffocated in them, she said, and the rates were outrageous. Whom did Emma like? Ernest, he thought, and something in him grinned. Turning from that thought as though it were a thing that stood and looked at him, he walked rapidly down the incline to the Palladino house.

A light from the kitchen cast a faint ray through the soiled windows. Mrs. Palladino was sitting at a cluttered table eating a piece of toast that looked painted. George knocked at the door. After a moment he looked in the window; Mrs. Palladino had not moved, although her eyes were fixed on the door, the toast held halfway to her mouth. He knocked again, then jumped to the window to see what she would do. She put the toast down on a salt shaker, tried to balance it, then stared at it. She was crazy.

He didn't know why he wanted to see her anyhow. He was backing away, angered by her self-absorption, when she got up and came toward the door. As it opened, she thrust her narrow head out.

"Excuse me," George said.

Mrs. Palladino laughed. "Have you been peeing on the roses?" she asked. There were no roses, only the shards of a broken milk bottle. She was clutching the door frame.

He stood there silently while the door opened wider. He couldn't think why he was standing there.

"Oh, it's you," she said. "Did you want to come in here? You can come in if you want."

The smell of the kitchen undid him. It was foul—sour milk, whiskey, stale tobacco, rotting things, the queer, dead sweetness of detergent spilling from a box on the floor. Was he going to cry?

"Sit down," she said, waving him toward a bench at the table. "I'm eating. I'm sobering up." And she laughed again.

"Emma just left me—the house," he said. "My wife . . ."

She sat silently a minute, looking down at the table; then, "What did you expect?"

Was it an accusation? Had Emma been running to her with stories?

"Wait—" he began.

"No, no . . ." she muttered, as she picked up the abandoned toast. She bit into it and chewed with an expression of strain and concentration. "I only mean to say, why are you so surprised?" A crumb fell from her lip. "You sounded surprised. Why is everybody so astonished in this goddamn place about what happens?"

"Stop playing dead," he said. "What do you think I feel?"

162

"If you'd have one drink with me, I'd only have one."
She looked up at him. "Jesus! A human face!" The
awful fragment of charred bread, yellow in spots, from
yesterday's buttering probably, fell to the floor. "Please,"
she said.

He nodded, and she was on her feet, away, and back in
a minute with a bottle of rye and two jelly glasses. She
filled them. He watched her take a small sip, her lips compressed. After she had put down the glass, she reached
across the table and took his hand in hers, its plumpness
girdled by her thin fingers.

"Darling," she said lovingly, and his heart felt as
though she had squeezed it. "I don't know if you feel much
of anything."

He lay quietly, as it were, in her hand, wanting to stay
there. Then she released it and took another sip.

"You don't know what happened," he said.

"The story depends upon the angle of vision."

"You're goddamned full of it. . . ."

"And that's the truth," she said.

Would she call him "darling" again? It had been so
startling, so sweet. Gratitude because he was drinking with
her. . . . He might have been anyone. No, there would be
no more darlings. With an impulse of malice, he silently
evoked his sister's name. Lila had made her suffer—she
couldn't fool him about that—and suffering is always a
surprise.

She bowed her head suddenly. "Well, what did happen?"

"I took in a boy I thought I could help. Ernest Jenkins.
Ernest. He laid my wife this afternoon."

She looked at him thoughtfully, then drank the rest of

her rye. "That boy . . . I saw him. Were you afraid of him?"

"Where the hell are you?"

"Let's have a bit more."

"I took him into my house."

"I don't know what you're talking about." She was pouring out rye, grinning, a fool.

"Cut it out," he shouted.

"You're lying."

"She told me."

"Listen. I didn't mean about that. What I mean is—the thing itself doesn't matter to you. Only the idea . . . offensive, ugly, silly. You know what you look like? A piece of office furniture. You've got a grievance. Passion is something else."

He stood up. She shrank away from him at once, her eyes on his face. He saw her narrow shoulders, the putty-colored flesh, the drinker's rose, a mock stigmata high up on one cheek, the dying fall of beauty in her face, and he let his hand fall to his side and sat down. She filled his glass and drank humbly from her own. He thought he heard a child cry out, but when he looked at her questioningly, she shook her head. "A dream . . ." she said, and asked him, "Do you like what you do?"

"I don't know now," he said.

She nodded, and he felt vaguely flattered. All right, if she wanted him to know nothing, he would know nothing. Perhaps that was her idea of truth: things must not be named; not-knowing. Playing her game, he began to feel better.

"Is Joe here?"

"He's with that dumb sister of yours."

164

"I'm sorry."

"You're sorry," she mocked.

"But there's more to it than that, isn't there?" he asked, getting some of his own back.

"Thanks."

"Doesn't it bother you?" he asked; then suddenly, "Why do you make me feel like a crook?"

She felt among a pile of papers at the end of the table and took out two scraps and handed them to him.

"She writes him at the Guild office. He leaves things around. I used to think he wanted me to find all those letters and notes and even little drawings. But now, I think he doesn't even know what he's doing."

George recognized Lila's hurried scrawl. "How rich other peoples' lives are, I've always thought," she had written, "and how neglected, inept and futile mine has been until now."

He let it drop on the table. Lila's little cheesecloth bits of disguise. Definitions. On the other piece, only two words were scrawled, "Oh, Joe—" He looked up to see Mrs. Palladino looking at him intently.

"That was the one," she whispered. "The other is nothing. But that one made me sick. I know what it felt like—to write that, to receive it. He doesn't really care about her, you know, but that was a dagger. The power of longing . . . you see? The power . . ."

"But why do you stay?" he asked, no longer really curious. A monumental sadness had settled upon him.

"We have perfected our dance," she said.

But he had no time to listen. Something was closing in. Yet he was irritated by what she had said. A small irritation, like an insect bite.

"A dance . . . that's only a name for something," he said.

"I name it all. To make plans out of accidents. You've been doing it now, yes, you weren't there with her and the boy, with Jenkins, but you're naming it, aren't you?"

"There are plenty of words for that," he said, and laughed suddenly, bending over the table, seeing a week of her life in saucers and cups and plates. "*Mea culpa* is one."

"There's an end to saying that," she said. He was thinking that he had never written a letter to anyone which evoked only their name—it had never come upon him that way.

"I should have known," he said.

"I don't even like Joe any more," she said. "But every day it gets harder to think of changing things."

"They did it against me—bad children."

"Children," she echoed. "The children are here, reminding of another time."

"She behaved as if I had been the one who had outraged *her*. How can they feel self-righteous when they've been so dirty?"

"*They!*" she said. "Listen to you!"

"Some people," he said, "cannot endure life unless they feel themselves blameless down to their fundaments."

"You're envious," she said and laughed. "Fundament. The ass may indeed be innocent."

He turned his glass over. "Do you drink all the time?"

"No. But I *feel* as though I'm drunk all the time. I called Joe a male cow yesterday. It was so meaningless when the words came together, before I said them, but when we both heard what I said, it was awful. I don't even know what

I meant." She hit the table with her hand. "I'm so sick of it! Thinking about myself. Loathsome! Even when I tend to the little girls, I'm thinking—here I am, their mother, taking care of them."

He shuddered. "I wanted to be concerned with Ernest. That was the whole thing."

"Was it?" she jeered.

"Guru! Oracle . . ."

"Those are birds that fly backwards, aren't they?" she asked, and smiled.

He stood up, wanting to leave, to be away from the country silence. He noticed how closely she watched him stand, the way an invalid might, thinking himself unobserved.

"Where are you going?" she asked.

"To New York. To see my friend, Walling, a painter." He had not thought of Walling until that moment, neither as a friend nor as a painter.

"Will you sit for your portrait?" she asked, moony now.

"He's a teacher," he said, hearing himself, the old priggishness in his voice, the fear of misrepresenting. "He teaches mathematics." He wondered what a portrait of himself would look like, unable to imagine his face, thinking instead of the clothes he would wear; it would be a portrait of a suit, a teacher's suit. He laughed irritably— the twisting burrows his thoughts dragged him through.

"A teacher . . ." she said, abstracted.

"I don't know. . . . I must go now." He touched her cheek with one finger; her skin was damp, as though with exertion. Clumsily, she kissed his hand.

"You need to put on weight," he said.

"I'm scared of everything," she said. "Silence and noise, open windows, shut doors." Then she scowled. "As if everybody wasn't scared," she muttered.

George recognized the sound of an interior dialogue, stale, lonely, without end.

"Good night," she said with a profound sigh which he knew had nothing to do with him.

"Good night . . ."

Traveling at night has a mysterious urgency. Signs of human habitation appear—a yellow lamp in a window, a white fence—and sink at once into obscurity.

A vast, deserted station platform, the highway at this hour was emptied of commuters; only now and then a car going north passed George, or there was a faint flicker of light from behind reflected in his rearview mirror.

Expecting misery now that he was alone, expecting a preoccupation with Emma and Ernest, George felt instead the pleasures of car and empty road and night. Was that all there was to it? He wasn't so sure now that he would bother to look up Walling. He probably wasn't even in the city. But the thought of his portrait persisted and he strained to catch a glimpse of himself in the mirror. He saw nothing but the thumbed-out features of a face seen through a window at night.

The sensation of freedom, brought on perhaps because he wasn't sure where he was going, rose and ebbed. His own face, emptied, nagged at him. Pumpkin, office furniture.

Women wanted blood and death on the face—forgiveness in the heart. He was supposed to look like what had happened to him. Lila had tormented him; he had cheated her by looking like a pumpkin. Didn't they know under-standing had its own procedures—and that he didn't understand? He could hardly give himself an illusion of sequence; the events which had taken place were terrible because they seemed random, inexplicable.

He suddenly visualized Joe Palladino, his lifeless hair coming alive around his neck and curling like a dog's. "Oh, Joe—" Lila had written. The car lurched as George's foot came down on the accelerator. It was that that would drive him crazy, that sexual cry! Was Martha looking at the note again, touching it?

How could he care about Emma and her furtive screw-ing—cold and nervous and angry. Aware that he was traveling at seventy miles an hour, he slowed down. He wouldn't die for it, he thought, not sure what he meant, as though his real thoughts were taking place in another language whose key eluded him.

He came to Hawthorne Circle and saw a police car hidden by trees. He wondered if the Devlins ever felt criminal. Was the nearest you could come to happiness a feeling of unqualified self-justification? If that were true, probably the Devlins had attained bliss. He turned slowly into the Saw Mill River Parkway; the police weren't look-ing at him, but still . . . He wondered what time it was, but he had left his watch somewhere. Anyway, time was for the kitchen—kitchen time, meals, little moppings and wipings.

Now he wished he were driving north, not toward the city, New York, the hubcap of the world.

At the Henry Hudson Bridge, he missed the toll station coin receptacle and had to get out of the car and hunt for his dime as out of the corner of his eye he saw a policeman

169

lumber toward him. There was a gargle of machinery as he dropped the dime in; the green light went on. Saved again!

Brilliant through the city's night haze, the George Washington Bridge, beaded throughout its length with light, clamped New York to the mainland.

Why not cross over? A vague memory stirred of those Jersey smells, as vivid as the colors they evoked. He and Lila and Mama had driven to Philadelphia once, hadn't they? To see a relative? Was it a funeral? He couldn't remember the purpose of the trip, only the back seat of the car, gray, scratchy, himself huddled in a corner, *their* prisoner, Lila's and his mother's, their heads straight and stiff in front of him, never turning back, lit by the ghastly light of the gas fires starting up out of the swamp through which they were traveling, the great hump of a bridge rising, the Pulaski Highway, Skyway? Was that it? It had terrified him, yet he had giggled. "Hush!" his mother had said. Then she had cried, "So messy!" Meaning him? Meaning that landscape of perpetual catastrophe through which they drove? Messy.

He supposed she had been afraid too, that strange old woman, her hands gripping the steering wheel as they climbed up the incline of the bridge, feeling God knows what beating at her back, alone, two children growing up like enemies.

Would Ernest know that George knew now what had taken place in the spare room. But, oh God, he *didn't* know! He could see him, hands in his pockets, white face above a dark shirt, standing somewhere, alive now. Snake. Afraid the car would somehow be informed of his anger, he slowed down to a crawl. A horn trumpeted behind him.

Naturally Emma had to let Ernest climb on her to show she was a man even if her husband wasn't. He shouted with laughter.

Keeping pace with him in a battered touring car were three Negro boys. They were laughing too, pointing at him and shaking their heads. George rolled down his window.

"Fuck you!" he shouted across the wind, still laughing.

"Mutha—" cried the one next to the window. "Live it up, baby!"

Just to his right was the Ninety-sixth Street exit. He waved to the boys and turned off the highway, driving north and east until he came to his school. Ugly, substantial, it dominated the south side of the block. He let the motor idle as he sat there staring at the darkened windows of the building.

That's where he got money. The last week of every month a salmon-colored check was left in his mailbox by Daddy Claus. Every month he took it off to the bank, made out a deposit slip, faced life, wrote checks.

He remembered Freddie Maas, whom he had known in college. Freddie had sold all his books to get the money to have his floors sanded and stained. Maas had been close to the end of his Ph.D. thesis. George, stopping by to see him, had found Maas standing in the middle of the room, staring down at his black walnut floor. "How about that?" he had said. And George, thinking Maas's moral energy had collapsed, or else he'd gone mad, had asked timidly, "What about Thomas Hardy?" "T. Hardy can go take a galloping fuck at himself," Maas had said. "I don't want it. I just don't want any part of the whole thing."

171

George had heard later that Maas had gotten some sort of administrative job with an oil company in Saudi-Arabia. Sand. All of a piece.

In the Northwest Territories there were one-room schoolhouses to which the Canadians, it was said, would fly a teacher, and pay him ten thousand dollars for one year. Indians. Wolves. He could teach in a blanket. A cot near a stove—open the door, walk into the classroom. No bathing, wolf stew. Why not? And the year after that he could go to Afghanistan. They had American schools there, didn't they? Skiing in the winter, swimming pools, love on a plateau, lots of money, no taxes. And after that?

A police car idled beside him; one of the policemen was eating a hard-boiled egg. Two faces looked at him impassively, one chewing. He realized he was hungry. He drove on. In six weeks, the school would open its doors. Mecklin of the Northwest Territories would ascend the steps, drawn there by the contract he had made with himself years ago.

He drove to the East Side, remembering Walling had given him an address on East Tenth Street. They could eat together somewhere. He didn't want to eat alone. Whenever he and Emma had gone to a restaurant, he had always been uncomfortably aware of the solitary diners. Weren't they embarrassed? Lonely? It had not occurred to him until now that they might be eating alone from choice, or from a whole sequence of choices which had led them to one plate, one glass, one opened newspaper, a book.

Well, he wasn't ready to eat alone yet. There would be time enough for that. He would divorce Emma for juvenile adultery and give her the car. He would divorce his sister

172

while he was at it. And he would divest himself of house and property and books, especially books. Freedom was a public library.

He found he had reached Twenty-third Street, and he wondered briefly how he had driven so far without being aware of driving. What took over? He glanced at the gas gauge. It was half full; he had been more careful than he thought. He always was, in small matters. Someone was honking furiously. He stalled. But it wasn't for him that the horn blew. A bus had stopped; other cars hesitated, although the light was green. He saw a flurry of movement on the corner. A police car was parked next to another car which was nosed up against a fire plug, and a policeman standing there held a tape measure. Just beside the door of the car, her arms held tightly across her chest, a woman watched. George started up and inched forward. The policeman began to measure the angle between the car and the curb; a broken headlight lay on the pavement. The woman must have damaged city property; the excitement, what there was of it, was administrative, not medical. For a wild moment, George thought she was Emma. But this woman was much older. Perhaps it had been the alarm on her face that had reminded him of Emma. A crowd had gathered; they ate the woman up with their eyes. Strangers in trouble were mysterious, entertaining.

It might have been he who had had the accident, or something worse—killed a child, run down an old man familiar to the neighborhood.

Now he wanted to see Walling desperately and in the intensity of his desire was convinced Walling would not be anywhere in the city. Walling's address was written down on the slip of paper he had found in his wallet. The

173

worn leather felt gritty; looking at the words and numbers in the uneven light which came through the car window, George felt vaguely furtive. The writing was that of a stranger; even as he stared at it, it lost meaning, seemed cabalistic. That was the afternoon he had seen that girl whom he had found so distasteful. Thinking of her, of Emma, of all the people he knew, he felt barely alive, as though each one held some essential element of himself which he could not reclaim.

Near St. Mark's Place he found a parking place. Just as he got out of the car, two men staggered across the street supporting each other with what appeared to be empty sleeves. Other people's suits, he supposed.

Walling's studio was in a tenement. The mailbox panel —no names on it—looked recently bombed. Despite the gloom of neglect, George felt as he climbed the narrow stairs a sense of presences embedded in the dirty walls. He met no one; the stairs wound up and around, the chambers of a sea shell. On the top floor at the end of the passage was a red door, Walling's name painted on it in black letters. George knocked. There was no response although he could hear voices, children's voices. Nothing happened. He pushed, and the door opened.

The light inside was sick, the color of guano, pulsating as though the atmosphere were straining to purge itself. Lifeless variations of gray emanated randomly from the large, curved surface of a television screen. Blobs of creatures tumbled about in this quivering gelatin, speaking in voices that were almost human. The light, as it flickered over a collapsed leather chair, the cluttered floor, the dark head of a man, expressed a panic not so much human as electronic.

"Walling?"

"Here."

"George Mecklin."

"I'm watching *Reunion* with Jean Hersholt and the Dionne Quintuplets. A beautiful film."

Vestless, wearing a sweat shirt, his face darkened by a scruffy beard, his mustache drooping, Walling stared intently but without recognition at George. "It's nearly over," he said menacingly. He turned back to the screen, hunched over and clasped his hands between his knees. "Sit down," he muttered. "Don't miss the show. . . ."

George pulled a stool near the chair and sat, catching a strong smell of whiskey. Everybody was drunk. Everybody *he* knew was drunk. He felt like an invalid, thin, wasted, and, with an invalid's worry, wondered when he would be fed.

The picture on the screen was dissolving, as were the actors, weeping gummily.

"Christ!" Walling shouted. "This tube . . ." He flung himself at the set and began to grapple with it, grunting as he heaved it back and forth. "There's one tube that cuts off. . . . Can't be bothered with that thief and his little goddamn box of parts every time this thing . . ." He slammed a knee into the side and with a kind of belch, the light came back.

"Listen . . ." George said.

"Go ahead," Walling said. "Now look! We missed the reunion. Pricks! Sorry . . . I can't turn it off. No lights here. I keep forgetting to get a bulb. If I turn the sound down, we can see all right. Look at that goat shit they're peddling! See that woman? She's got no orifices, all plugged up. This country's going to explode. I used to know a man, when somebody died, he'd say, 'There goes Charlie! He blew up.' Could you run down to the corner and get me a bottle of bourbon? Here . . ." Walling held out some bills. George stood up.

"Why, George!" cried Walling. "For Christ's sake, it's you!" He grabbed George by his shoulders, rocking him back and forth; he lifted him a foot off the ground, dropped him and then fell back into the leather chair.

"I didn't know you'd be here. I thought you were going away."

"I never go away. Never go. . . ."

The ghastly light brightened. The small room was stuffed with things, all dominated by the leather chair and the television set. Canvases leaned against the walls; an easel seemed to advance toward George on its wooden struts; lined up on a table were dozens of grapefruit-juice cans from the tops of which brushes obtruded—in these nauseous shadows, the brushes looked like a horde of spectators, a cartoon crowd. A hot plate with a coffeepot on it stood on a suitcase, and near it was a cot, a coat flung over it.

"Here. You want to see my work?" Walling hoisted himself up, rushed to a group of canvases and pulled out a few. He held each one in front of the television screen for a few seconds.

"You'll have to come here before you can see them . . . best way to look . . . inaction painter, why not? My own collective unconscious. Not as good as the box here, right? I suffer from this greediness with purple. It always lets you down. This one's a portrait of my wife. No, it's a lamp. I bought it for a quarter from a fairy around the corner. . . ."

The paintings had a dreary similarity: muddy paint had been laid on canvas with a palette knife, swollen circles bulging on one side like diseased tires. Walling heaved them back into the corner, one by one.

"If we're going to have a drink, you'll get it, won't you?"

"I'm hungry."

"Fine. We'll go to the Ticino. Lemon veal. You want to go to the Ticino? In the next village, not far at all."

"Anyplace."

"That's a poor statement. Helpless. Be a man, choose a restaurant."

"I didn't know you were married."

"I'm not now. You want the last of this? Hardly one drink left. Thanks, then . . . I'll have it. Glad you dropped in."

"My wife took off . . . permanently." George had meant to say she had left him, but he was suddenly ashamed. Perhaps he should have argued about the restaurant.

Walling was laughing. He choked, coughed without restraint, laughed again.

"Don't take them to the country," he said. "After the bread is made and the curtains hung, they start getting sore."

"I didn't say she was sore."

"They're always sore. What do you mean, she wasn't sore? Who's laughing. You ought to hear what happened to me. I don't even want to talk about it. Or did you mean she went off her rocker?" Walling frowned as he tore a long strip of leather from the arm of the chair and threw it at the set.

"Look! They're trying to get to me. Look. How she is straining! Oh, Gladys, darling . . . sell me your darling hair ick . . . oh! its sweet teeth, itsy bitsy dirl person, connect at joints, press buzzer, mouth opens."

"Why did you laugh?"

"Ignore what I do. It's all reflex. The only woman I've ever liked is a Catholic virgin of thirty. She's superior. Her nonsense electrifies me."

"I liked Emma," George said, and knew as he said it that he lied. He hadn't liked her at all.

Walling stood, swaying. "I hate to turn it off," he said waving at the television screen, then he did and they stood silently in the dark. Walling sighed heavily. "Although it *is* something one can turn off," he said.

They walked west and south, passing buildings where men slept in doorways, above them windows marked with giant white X's like letters in a child's alphabet. Sometimes Walling fell against George, then straightened himself and thrust his head forward with the passionate, blurred resolution of drunkenness. He took hold of George's arm and gripped it and began to speak of Alicia.

"I was crazy—trying to get all the degrees at once. I wanted to get it over with, you understand? Get a job, a check, a name for what I was doing in the world. Besides, my uncle Sol was on my back. I was a Jew once, yes, who else has an Uncle Sol? He was paying for all of it because my father was dead . . . he felt obligated. Sol the rhinoceros, puffing and huffing and kicking up the dirt, stomping around in his compound . . . but he paid. Alicia was writing a thesis on *Orlando Furioso,* bird imagery, and she spoke Italian—it was not to be believed, her ear for languages. Turn right here."

"Where are we?"

"Never mind. Listen. I'll get you there. She woke me up once at three a.m. to sing me a Chinese opera. Oh, not real Chinese, gibberish, but so exactly like the feeling of it I thought I'd die laughing. She was freakish, like those birds you train to make human sounds. She could learn any language in six weeks. I was out of my mind, exalted, depressed. . . . She was very fair, pale, long legs. In the afternoons, I'd meet her in a bar. I'd stop at the entrance to look at her for a moment—took my breath away. Those sharp Protestant elbows leaning on the table, her ankles, bare elegant bones bent, just so, beneath the table. This is how she'd greet me—with a sentence in Russian, French, Italian, Spanish, Portuguese. It was like a circus train all strung together on one track."

Walling's grip tightened, and George wondered if he'd made some involuntary movement to escape him.

"Listen—" Walling urged. "Listen! She wasn't—" He stopped speaking suddenly and looked up at the windows of a large apartment house which had been thrust in among the runty, collapsing tenements. "The consumers," he muttered. "The consumers!" he shouted.

George waited beside him, miserable, waiting for the police, for flowerpots to be dropped on his head.

"I started to explain," Walling continued conversationally, walking on, "that she wasn't observably middle-class. Not bohemian either. Odd, displaced."

"Are we far?"

"Almost there," replied Walling.

"I'm not listening to you," George shouted suddenly. "How can I? I'm too damn hungry. What's all this about?"

Walling snorted. "Why George! How are you going to

179

get me to listen to you if you don't hear me out? Quid pro crap! I've irritated you, haven't I? Alicia said that was the only way I knew how to *relate* to people, when she began to speak English exclusively, that is. Relate! Terrible language. When I couldn't bear getting into bed with her any more, she used to arrange herself in a chair and talk about the need for *skin contact*. My God. I was too embarrassed not to listen. Now comes the funny part. I had this very fat friend, Billy; we'd knocked around together for years. When Alicia and I were married, he was the witness. In fact, we really married him. He found us an apartment, arranged the furniture and cooked for us. Things went to hell fast. She hated getting up in the morning. He told me it was because we weren't suited to each other. He'd never thought so, he said. After seven years of Riker's orange juice and brutally fried food, without a quiver all that time, my stomach suddenly went to pieces. If Billy didn't cook dinner, we ate stuff from cartons. I was always running to the bathroom in the middle of a fight. When I'd get back in the living room, he'd be there, handing her a cup of herb tea—so they both said. How do I know what it really was? He spoke a little French too, the dirty bastard! As this psychotic idyll drew to a close, she took to calling everything Mister—like, 'Oh, look! There's Mister Squirrel!' or 'Mister Policeman.' It drove me wild, as if she were calling me filthy things in baby talk. I used to try to trick her into speaking other languages —ask her how to say this or that. All this time I was teaching, my first job, and coming home to them. He'd be wearing one of her bitty aprons, his fat, white voice going on and on about what he'd found in *Gourmet* magazine. She'd say to me, of course it wasn't kosher food like I used to. . . ."

He jumped sideways suddenly, so that he was standing directly in front of George. "One minute. We're nearly there. I can't stop now. One night I went out to a drug-store to get some antacid pills and I picked up a girl there. I stayed out late. When I came home, they were both in the kitchen, dirty coffee cups everywhere, smoking my cigarettes, talking about money—in *English*, pal! They were going to open a school, a language school. When I walked in, they both began to laugh. I broke everything in the kitchen."

"All right," said George. "It's a terrible story. Let's go."

"Do you really think it's terrible?" asked Walling almost hopefully.

"Yes."

"Next thing that happened, she began to talk about some suicidal cousin in Chicago. She just had to go and help the kid out. I assume old Billy went with her. While they were gone, that girl stayed with me. She was restful, hardly spoke any language. I wasn't careful—her things all over the place, notes. I suppose I wanted Alicia to know. And I think she went away just so it could happen. Well . . . she told me I'd broken the fifth commandment. I told her she wasn't up on her Old Testament. She said she'd expect a Jew to know it—how was she supposed to? A Christian and all that. Billy said I had no right to a beautiful and in-corruptible wife like Alicia."

They had crossed Washington Square and walked a block down Thompson Street.

"Is that the restaurant?" asked George.

"So that's what happened to me. Yes. That's the place."

"You got a divorce?"

"A long time ago."

They walked down a few steps and into a room with a number of tables, a monstrous air conditioner and a faded brown photograph of the *padrona* over the bar.

"We're closed," a waiter said. "The door shoulda been locked."

"Just a plate of *pasta* for my friend," asked Walling.

"Kitchen closed," the old man said sternly. "Go down the street. We're tired."

"I hate working-class self-righteousness," Walling said. The waiter picked up a chair and upended it on a table without a glance at the two men.

They walked up Bleecker Street. It was clotted with wanderers straggling along the sidewalk. Sometimes a group stopped to stare in through the open doors of bars; empty-eyed, restless, their bodies looked caved in, as though exhaustion had mutilated them. A Negro homosexual wearing a yellow turtle-neck sweater slipped along the edge of the curb; his steps were as pointed, as small as his black boots. He looked exquisite and afraid, yet on his down-turning face there was a sly smile, as though he were reading a message left for him on the pavement.

Walling talked on and on, about his life, his family. His father, he said, had not faltered once on his way to a fatal heart attack in his forties. "Jews and learning are a more complicated matter than you can imagine," he said.

"I can imagine."

"No. You can't. Learning for enlightenment and pleasure is entirely different from arming for battle."

George took Walling's arm and pulled him into a bar that advertised pizzas. They slid along the vaguely greasy benches of a booth.

"All through high school, he was thinking of college,"

Walling said. "All through college, he was thinking of graduate school. And then he was through. Where was the war? Where was the enemy? There was nothing. Nothing. That's why I hate Rubin."

Walling ordered a drink for himself from the waiter and when it had come, drank it down quickly and ordered another. "What it comes down to—Rubin wants to kill the world."

"Why do you hate him? I missed something. Don't you think you should eat?"

"You miss a lot, George," Walling said with some malice. "You know why I dislike my students? Because of my poor dumb dutiful old man. They sit there in all their insolence—which is just a refusal to learn—and I know they won't die of heart attacks because there is something in the world for *them*. I suppose they're right. Are they right, George?"

"I don't know. I don't hate them."

"But they bore you. That's worse. Still, boredom is a goy's privilege. Jews don't have time."

"You sound like Rubin. Speaking for everybody."

Walling hiccoughed. "I am reminded," he said, "of how I took to playing solitaire in the evenings. Alicia detested it. One night she said, 'When you lose a game, it's because I won it!' " He laughed, put his head down on his hands, then looked up at George. "How's that! Can you top that?"

George was gulping down a wedge of the pizza which had been placed between them. As his stomach filled, he felt a certain dull peacefulness.

"You remember too much," he said.

"Look at the young girls," Walling said, sitting up and

waving at the window. Outside on the street, two young women were peering through the plate glass. One was squinting aggressively; the other's eyes were opened dreamily as though what she saw was her heart's desire. Her mouth pouted. George marked its shape as if he had traced it with a finger. It was an ordinary human mouth, millions like it, puffy in the center of the lower lip. She was wearing that neurotic lipstick—it struck him that way —an off-red. But it was a pretty mouth. It would be undistinguished but absorbing to kiss her, soft, no response, but still, he wanted to, this moment, as she stood there in her nice clothes like something in a pillow, stitched up all around, gloved, hatted and girdled. All sewed up, ready to be ripped open.

He glanced back uneasily at Walling, but Walling was staring at the bar, where a huddle of people were shouting and laughing.

"I know that game," Walling said.

My game? wondered George. The girl was still there, abstracted, moony. Her friend had hold of her arm. George shuddered, groaned to himself, in pain. He wanted them all, sealed in their envelopes, lined up exclusively for him.

"It's Sicilian," Walling was saying. "Did you know that? Rock, scissors, stone. We used to play it. All those games are Italian."

"Not too hard, darling!" screamed a woman. Standing beside her, his fingers shaped into scissors, was the man who held her arm. All at once he brought his fingers down violently, snapping them against her skin. "You bastard!" she said. The group of people grew silent. Then one by one they turned back to the bar.

"I'm going to take you to a party," Walling said. "Let's get out of here."

George paid their bill while Walling dug ineptly in his pockets. "Your night," he muttered.

More streets; more faces which appeared to George stranger than those he had seen earlier, neither animal nor quite human, yet marked with a remote suffering—perhaps, he thought, they already knew that the night's pleasures which they so remorselessly sought would never materialize.

The first floor of the tenement to which Walling took him was paved with diamond-shaped tiles as gray as those on the floors of public toilets. They slowly climbed five flights of stairs. A dog barked from behind a green door. Party noise broke in incoherent waves against the walls. The door was open. They walked into a kitchen, the walls of which were covered with painted arrows pointing in all directions. A police lock slid along the floor. Drawn on the door was a cartoon man, his lumpy legs spread out just where the lock would have fitted into place.

A reddish-haired, plump man was carving ham efficiently, an expression of restrained but somewhat theatrical impatience on his face as several women giggled and fluttered around him, touching his back, his shoulders, exclaiming at the determined downward slice of the knife. He was wearing a small organdy apron. Now and then he stopped carving and looked around at the women with an air of comic disbelief. "The line between chic and murder is very blurred these days," he said to George and Walling.

In each of the three other small rooms men and women and others leaned toward each other; some sat on the floor. A middle-aged woman looked desperately at a shelf of books. Walling left George by himself and went to the farthest room. George talked aimlessly with a few people: a drunken young lawyer who was holding a flat gold watch at which he glanced from time to time; a Negro couple, he a social worker, she an actress with a slender, cool face; a dark-haired, thick-legged woman who clutched his arm and told him she had just given up smoking because she wanted to savor every minute of her life. She leaned against him hopefully, but he didn't want to be savored.

Walling appeared suddenly at his side. "I've got to have some Chinese food," he said, dragging George back to the kitchen. "They're starting to play Vivaldi. . . ."

The reddish-haired man was chopping up a Chinese cabbage.

"Thanks," said Walling.

"How've you been?" asked the man, his eyes swimming. Onions? Alcohol? Grief?

"Impeccable," said Walling.

"Same old bullshitter, aren't you, Harve? Civilization is extenuating circumstances. My own." He dropped the cabbage into a bowl, then turned and whacked the buttocks of a young woman in a blue dress. As George and Walling walked out the door, the man called out, "I hear Alicia is living in Yugoslavia."

"Oh, Christ . . ." Walling said.

They took a taxi to George's car. From there Walling directed him uptown to One Hundred and Twenty-fifth Street. "It'll be closed," George said.

"Never closes. . . ."

George was feeling sick. He had drunk several glasses of white wine; the pizza seemed to have re-formed just under his ribs.

186

He parked the car under the huge Tinker Toy of elevated tracks. As they got out, a subway raced above them. After the thunder had subsided, the street was menacingly silent except for the small click and hum of the traffic lights as they changed from green to red. A light wind beat up One Hundred and Twenty-fifth Street from the river, where the remains of the old Hudson River Day Line docks rose, an inexplicable barrow now. The Chinese restaurant was closed.

"It never closes," said Walling sadly, looking at the dark windows.

From the entrance of a ramshackle building next to the restaurant a young boy suddenly appeared. He ran up to George.

"Hey, Mister. You want to see a dead man?"

Startled, George laughed. "I've seen enough," he said. The boy stared at George, puzzled, his arm pointing back at the doorway.

"No. I mean a real, live dead man. . . ."

George and Walling walked back to the car. When George looked back, the boy had disappeared.

"Some drunk . . ."

"Maybe we ought to have gotten the police," George said.

"Shut up," said Walling. "Let's go back to Tenth Street. You can have the cot. I'll take the chair. Maybe there's a late movie full of dead people. Everything is so unsatisfactory. I'll have to go to sleep hungry."

"Why don't you settle for ham and eggs?"

"I don't intend to settle."

"You're sure you don't want to stop somewhere?"

Walling was slouched down in the seat, his knees

crammed against the dashboard. If George hadn't been looking at him, he wouldn't have seen Walling nod. Inconsiderate bastard, thinking people would look at him in time to catch his languid affirmations.

"I didn't know you lived there."

Walling grunted. "You sound so—stretched. My dream hovel! My twenty-seven-inch screen! Summer dreams . . . When September comes, I'm a different man. I have a two-room apartment, George, right in that center of capitalist realism, Lincoln Square. An old lady comes once a week to vacuum my green rug and clean out my rotten sinks. I even have closets with my clothes hanging straight, and an ash tray by my bed." He paused, then said petulantly. "That *studio* . . . The operational principle is survival. That's why I left her to him. But no matter what people say—how they've hated each other for years, all that—it's *always* terrible. That's not apparent right away. First, I was relieved. I floated free. That purified air. I struggled with it for a few weeks, then rushed back and threw myself on the floor in front of her. I needed help, she said. She knew a charming little analyst. Or Billy knew one. I forget. So I went—cunningly. You see, I thought she was making a rendezvous with me. I told myself she was a prisoner and had contrived a plan so we could meet secretly."

"Did you like the analyst?"

"Like him! George, you great booby!"

"If you think I know what the hell you're talking about . . ."

"I went to him for a year," Walling continued. "It's because of him I rented that craphouse on Tenth Street. He told me to move, to take up something, anything. For months, I continued to think she would meet me at his office. I was always early so I wouldn't miss her. She phoned me every week . . . to see how I was. Yugoslavia. My God, what's she doing there?"

Was Walling being ironic? What was he being? If A is not B, it must be C. When something wasn't clear, it was only because one hadn't grasped the sequence. But that wasn't so either. How was one to know what A was? A might be a thought, a thing, a shadow of either. Walling's voice, alternately thick and watery, had begun to grate on George.

"I rented out my apartment in the summer so I could pay for the studio. Alicia hasn't phoned for months. I'm thinking about marrying that Catholic woman. Not yet though."

Walling had turned around; George could feel that he was watching him. The expectation seemed clear; he was now to tell about himself, but he couldn't. Only a few hours ago it had been possible for him to say something to Martha Palladino. He couldn't remember what he had said. It was already too late. The truth lay among its own shattered fragments. His head hurt; he felt as though an obscure part of his body was suffering, but the nature of the pain, its locus, eluded him.

"I can't feel it!" he cried out suddenly.

And Walling, as though George had enunciated some universal principle, groaned and clapped his hands to his face. He didn't speak until George had parked the car. "I'll marry her when I give up the studio," he said, as George bent over to lock the door.

Once back in the room, Walling turned on the television set, then fell into the leather seat, his head sunk between his shoulders, his eyes fixed on the silent screen.

George lay down on the couch. There was some hard

object just beneath the small of his back. He didn't bother to remove it. A book, probably. He began to feel oddly small, as though he had been rendered in a crucible and had lost most of his adult weight. And feeling small, he felt an anguished loneliness, the helpless loneliness of childhood. He peered at Walling, but he was already asleep, his face streaked by the unearthly television light. A distant mutter of voices emanated from the set like a conversation in another room. What comfort was there anywhere? He had taken his wretchedness to two people only to remind them of their own.

Something was gathering in the darkness around him, unimaginable, disastrous. George sat up. He must get back to his house. There was no paper and no pencil to leave a note, and there were no words to explain his urgency. He crept out into the dark hall.

He drove from city streets to the highway, where only gasoline stations threw up a momentary acid heat, and then into the country night. By then he was somewhat tentatively prescribing for himself—a week for cleaning out the house, getting ready to move back to New York, then preparation for the opening of school. What point could there be in staying on in the country? Expending so much effort for a gray winter's landscape and a squalid little house? He would have to see Emma at some point; somebody would have to see her. Money, law, papers, checking accounts.

Hours ago he had driven south on the same road which now, no longer obscured by the simple desperation with which he had driven on it earlier, seemed personal to him, as though it led to an end exclusively his own.

Driving at night—for him it was basic, archetypal, essential. Had he experienced it any differently on his first night's journey alone when he had driven on the old country road to Provincetown one summer fourteen years ago? Then, as now, the wheeled box had relieved him of his bodily concerns. From beginning to journey's end, he had been the spirit of the engine. Certainly it was a new thing under the sun, this kinship with cars. It was a kind of possession. He had heard that in Milan of a Sunday, it was possible to count sixty wrecks within fifteen miles of the city.

That drive to Provincetown had been such a long time ago. How old had he been when through an inch of steamy train window he had seen the dark village adrift in the snow? Those were ultimate memories—not recollections —experienced anew each time they came to him. If he drove all night, perhaps they would all come back, the primordial stuff of his life. Nearly everything else, he thought, was information. Like everyone he knew, he had become more information than anything else.

Like everyone he knew? What about Martha, for whom the mantle of the commonplace had worn away? But what a hell of a way to be: hung between two absolutes, health or dissolution, loathing the one, deriding the other, inter- changeably probably. She was the person you met after an accident, a permanent mourner. He remembered how beau- tiful her arms had looked.

Thinking of hers, he remembered his mother's arms. One day, he had really looked at them. She had been wear- ing a sleeveless cotton blouse with a high collar. Between her armpit and her elbow, he had seen the arc of soft flesh, freckled, loose, a drape of flesh. In that same instant he had perceived that she was old. Somehow, she must have

191

known what he was thinking because she spoke to him sharply and sent him on some silly errand. She hadn't worn short sleeves again. But the sinful knowledge of death was already deeply lodged in him—the crochet hook puncturing the flesh, the shovel leaning into the snowbank. Everything died; death was eternal.

He drove across the bridge which crossed the Croton Reservoir, slowing down to turn off the Taconic State Parkway. For the first time he saw another car. It too had slowed down. A light went on and he saw a group of young men huddled together in the front and back seats. One was holding up a bottle which he lifted and drank from. The light went off; with an elderly gargle, the car slid away. Perhaps Ernest had been in there with the others. George thought not. Ernest wouldn't drink; he had to watch.

He came to a fork; the right road led to his house. What if Ernest were there waiting for him? What if he could never rid himself of Ernest? Feeling a sudden and violent distaste for those empty rooms—he knew damn well Ernest wouldn't come back now—he took the left fork, which led to the Devlin house. Without thinking much about anything, he parked the car a few yards from the Devlin driveway.

Lights were on all over the house except for one window on the south side. Making no effort to hide himself, George crossed the lawn, going toward the living-room windows. There was a rasp of insects. Moths were clustered on the screens in attitudes of supplication. There wasn't a breath of wind, only that curious suspension of motion that comes in late summer when everything seems poised on the edge of critical change. The moon had waned, but the stars were bright; flung across unimaginable distances, their lights were those of a reversed city.

The insect noise abated. George stood a few feet from the window which gave onto the living room. He unbuttoned the top of his shirt, feeling constricted by his clothes, and dirty, as though the city streets, Walling's room, the pizza bar had contaminated him.

If only he could fling off all his clothes! At the thought, he felt intensely nervous. He stared into the living room.

A large vase of wilting yellow flowers stood in the hearth where last he had seen burning logs. On a table in front of the window he saw a box from the top of which excelsior curled and spilled. Next to the box, as though to explain it, was a many-faceted goblet to which a few wisps of excelsior clung.

"What did you tell him?" asked Minnie's voice. George jumped back. She was sailing toward the window wrapped in a quantity of thin green silk, her face expressionless. She bent over the box, her hands scrabbling passionately as though her entire being had slid into her fingertips. She grunted, carefully extracted another goblet, pursed her lips to blow off the dust and set the goblet down next to the other, then stood back and stared at them. She turned, as though listening.

"I said, what did you tell him?" She looked down at her bosom, flicked at something with a finger, pressed her chin back to see. Then she smiled. George smiled too. He was trembling; he wanted to laugh out loud. He clapped his hand over his mouth and moved farther back from the window. Minnie stood there, looking from goblets to breasts. There was a distant sound of water flowing. George ran around to the other side of the house and discovered Charlie Devlin brushing his teeth in a small bathroom.

He brushed with cold intensity, up and down, the prescribed technique, expressionless except for a ritualistic grimace at intervals. Big, strong, wolf teeth. He brushed, the spume dripping from the corners of his mouth, spots of paste flying at the mirror. Brush, brush . . . his teeth, not his teeth. Those choppers belonged to the world—to bite it, to grind it. A pinkish trickle of blood ran down Charlie's chin. He started forward, frowned, massaged his gum with the end of a towel and wiped the mirror with the same end. Then he washed out his brush, sighing audibly.

"I told them"—he bent forward again, dazzling himself with a toothed smile—"that if they hired that crapper to follow me around with an encyclopedia on his head, I'd quit. With or without facts, I told them, Charlie Devlin can talk about anything to anyone at any time. So they said how the hell could I run a series on existentialism without reading anything about it. So I told them I'd milked Kirkegaard dry in one reading. All I need to know is the first and last letter of any alphabet. The first and the last." He dropped the towel into a basket.

"Then they produced that disgusting little fairy with his crotch done up by faggot fashions, inc. and said he was at my service. All Ph.D., they said. I told them I had enough on my hands without having to watch my backside too."

Minnie appeared in the doorway. "In front of him?" she asked.

"I'm not without tact," said Charlie. He grasped his hips, swiveled around, narrowed his eyes. "Ootsie, tootsie, wootsie," he lisped.

194

"Well . . . you do have to put up with awful people, honey."

Charlie's hand suddenly shot out and grabbed Minnie in the region of her right breast. She screamed, laughed, backed away. They disappeared.

George lay down on the grass, pressing his face into its dampness. He heard his heart beat; an insect crawled across his nose. He got heavily to his feet. He was shaking with laughter. Without caution, he raced to the front of the house. The Devlins were looking down at the goblets.

"I know what you like," Minnie was saying as Charlie grasped two glasses. "Don't I always know what you like?"

"That's a fact," said Charlie, a remote expression on his face. "Anyhow they fired him and hired her. I won't even have to see her—research assistant."

"A girl?"

Charlie laughed and began to walk around the living room. Minnie trailed after him, a sharp listening look on her face. Round and round they wound among their things: sofas, ottomans, tables, lamps, drapes, magazines, baskets. Who was following whom? Then Charlie stopped.

"You know . . . I hear something."

Minnie paused just behind him. She looked toward the windows.

"Yeah. I hear something. Thought I had before."

"A dog."

"A dog?"

They stood silently. Minnie's hand caressed the arm of the sofa. George listened too.

"Maybe it's Trevor," she said.

"Trevor is sound asleep." Devlin turned to the windows, his back to Minnie. Minnie's hand rested, then her face gave the impression of swelling, as though filling up with an inrush of air; even her eyes bulged as her marble gaze rested on the back of her husband's head. If he had looked at her at that moment, George thought, he would have turned to stone.

But he did turn, and instantly Minnie smiled.

"A little country dog," she said, "out for fun and games."

Charlie scowled. "These towns around here are full of bums."

"Let's go to bed."

"Killers . . . You haven't seen the statistics." Charlie's eyes narrowed. The conviction of enemies seemed to give the human face its least ambiguous expression. How frightened Charlie looked! As he watched the fear intensifying, George remembered the feel of the door which had separated him from Ernest, remembered that first flash of pure terror which had riveted him to the door. Then Ernest had emerged. How easy it had been to forget that terror! To dissolve into benevolence! He had thought there was nothing that could resist understanding. What wantonness! He had tried to embrace Ernest only to keep Ernest's hands from his own throat. He had never felt a thing for Ernest, only fear.

Minnie had begun to turn out the lamps, leaning softly toward them, her fat hand curling around them with possessive lust, smiling as the lights went out. "Bed, bed, bed . . ." she sang. The room was suddenly dark.

They would probably go upstairs now. But George couldn't drop back into the night, not yet, back to his house, his lights and things and tasks. It was as though this strangeness he felt was not an emotion but a place he must have full knowledge of before he went back to his own life.

Then the hall light went off. George ran to the back of the house, around again, stumbling, backtracking, circling, his eyes straining to catch a ray of light that would show him where they had gone.

There had been a noise but he hadn't heard it. It came so suddenly he didn't know what was happening. He was sitting on the ground, the light from the open door falling full upon him. The Devlins ran toward him, Charlie holding out a gun, Minnie with her hands in her hair, screaming.

"Shut up!" howled Devlin. But she was screaming, "He's trying to untie his shoelaces! He's trying—" Charlie slapped her face with his free hand.

George, puzzled by his own sobbing, fumbled with his shoes; something pained his breast thickly; he had got his shoes on wrong again, and Lila and Mama were looking at him. One of them would say, "He doesn't even *feel* anything; even his feet don't tell him what a stupid he is!"

"Mecklin . . ." moaned Minnie. She turned suddenly, and George fell back into the grass. "Trevor's there!" she shouted. "You horrible bastard, you've let him see!"

"Call an ambulance," Charlie said, stooping over George. George looked up at him, aware now that he was bleeding, that a hole had been let into him, that Charlie had hidden his gun behind his back, that Charlie was growing taller and taller, like a tree taking root in George's breast where the pain was.

Chapter Six

ONE FLED back to the light; one stayed; then there were more figures. The longer blades of grass threw shadows on their legs.

"Is he conscious?" asked a voice from far away.

"As conscious as you are, Barney Google," replied one voice near George's ear.

"Ask where does he live?" said the first.

A shout—Charlie's: "I know where he lives!"

Intimately, as though it were inside his head, a voice moaned, "Why is he here?"

Minnie's fat ankles, dyed red by the taillight of the ambulance, quivered; a mosquito clung to one.

Charlie's face swooped down. *"Where is Emma?"* he demanded, as though speaking to a foreigner.

"Gone," whispered George.

An arm went around his shoulder. "I've got to seal you up. . . . You're open on both sides, see?"

"Help!" George cried as he was turned.

Minnie gasped.

"It's always larger where it goes out, lady."

Two unknown faces came close, one a Negro who asked: "You feel pretty bad?"

"Did he say Emma was *gone?*"

"*Shut up, Minnie!* Listen, I'll ride to the hospital with him. He's a friend."

"You always treat your friends this way?" asked the Negro, still leaning over George.

"Are you a doctor?" asked George, unable to hear his own voice.

"Maybe," said the Negro. George had never heard anything so mysterious; he looked meaningfully at the young man's face. But the Negro was looking at George's chest. "We're going to put you on a stretcher now, lift you up. Pretty soon you won't feel a thing."

"Let's go, Barney Google," said someone.

"Is that your name?" whispered George.

"God! What's he saying?" cried Minnie frantically. "Won't someone tell me?"

"It's not my name," the Negro said, on his knees, about to stand. "That's my buddy's joke."

"Kill him," George said, swirled into darkness, flying at terrible speed until he came back into light, smelling something ugly, conscious of a pillow under his cheek and Devlin squatting near.

"What the hell were you doing at the house? You know what time it is? How was I supposed to know it was you?"

"Don't talk to him."

"Why shouldn't I? He's conscious."

"Because I said not to."

The Negro's hand lay close to George's own. George took it weakly, holding on.

"Christ—" exclaimed Devlin.

"Don't talk," the Negro said to George. "We'll be there soon. They'll give you something nice, make you feel nice." He pressed George's hand, withdrew his own and turned his back to Devlin.

Lights fled across George's face, were gone in an instant. He heard traffic, saw the toppling roofs of buildings. The ambulance siren started up.

"Going to fall," George said. The Negro turned to him. George said, "The building . . ."

"No," said the Negro.

"Can I smoke?" asked Devlin.

"Now why do you ask me that?"

"Why not?"

"If you don't know why not, I can't tell you."

"Lousy regulations . . ."

"Get him out of here," George said in a creaking, new voice.

The Negro looked at Devlin. Devlin shrugged.

Then they arrived—a ramp, brown rubber rims on swinging doors, a corridor, smell of hospital, a room, two beds, a man on one groaning through the bandages that covered his face, a curtain half pulled around him but only hiding his legs. George was lifted, set down like broken crockery.

"What happened?" asked a man with a white cap covering his skull, bristles on chin and cheeks.

"I thought he was a prowler," said Devlin from nearby. "My God! You know what time it is? How would I know he'd come to visit at three in the morning?"

"You just came out shooting, huh?" That was the Negro.

"Why don't you go drop dead somewhere?" said Devlin.

"Take it easy," said the doctor. He bent over. "Just have to see," he said to George, his hand reaching toward the compress.

"Is he all right?" Devlin asked, his voice made out of some thick, vegetable substance.

"I don't know. . . ."

"You don't know?"

"If the lung collapses, it can push the heart over—tension pneumothorax. If blood or air get into the wall . . ." The doctor's voice was impatient. He wasn't young. George didn't take his eyes from the doctor's face—perhaps it would show him what was going to happen to him.

"But he's all right?" begged Devlin.

The doctor laughed in an unfriendly manner. "Yeah," he said. A policeman came up behind the doctor.

"What happened here, Sam?"

"I just got here," said the doctor irritably.

Devlin grabbed the policeman's arm. "He's a friend," he said. "A good friend. But he's got funny habits. You know, I couldn't tell who it was. Three in the morning—" The policeman shook off Devlin's hand and pushed him out into the corridor.

"Oh . . . oh . . . God . . ." groaned the man on the other bed.

"What happened to him?" asked George.

"You want a private room?" asked the doctor.

"No. It's beginning to hurt a lot."

"We'll give you something," said the doctor.

"What?"

The doctor scowled and turned away as he spoke to a nurse who was leaning against the door.

"I've got Blue Cross," said George wondering at his voice, so cracked, so childish.

"Congratulations," said the doctor. "Take him to 206," he said to the nurse. Then he leaned over George and smiled with an odd shyness, as though meeting him for the first time. "You'll be all right," he said. "We have to run a tube out of this . . . let the air escape. Don't make faces. You're lucky. He might have hit the other side."

"Mr. Mecklin," said the Negro, appearing at the side of the bed. "Is there anyone you'd like me to call?"

George shook his head. He had never been so tired in all his life. He wanted to thank the Negro for knowing his name. After you've been hurt, after the disaster, it was a sweet thing to hear your name. He was still here. Mr. Mecklin. He hoped he was smiling at the man, but he wasn't sure where his own face was.

Sickness made a child out of an adult; the present gave way, and there was the child alone at night. He looked about him with weak desperation for comfort, someone to touch him other than medically, remembering the clasp of the Negro's hand in the ambulance—and not finding it, he spoke too volubly to the intern who took down his medical history, smiled too much at the nurse who took his blood pressure, and grinned at them all as they ran a tube from the wound and another to a jar of glucose. His questions were ignored; his cheerful acceptance of pain not noticeably appreciated.

Perhaps, after all, they saw through him. The shakiness of his voice was not only shock but fear. What had been born in him was the knowledge of his own death. How could they assuage that fear? They knew it among themselves, the shared, ultimate secret of their profession

202

—beyond the necessity of what was required, why should they touch him? He was untouchable. The intern even looked at him accusingly, as though George's meager record had let him down; a tonsillectomy, for Christ's sake! A little sinus trouble; a mild urinary infection. Hardly distinguished.

The effect of the drug the nurse had given him had been intercepted by all the activity; there had been X rays and history, blood tests, sheet-folding, hands and machines at him. It would be a little while before he could have Demerol, the nurse said sternly, as if to forewarn him his complaints would do no good.

Then everyone left just as the pale, silver light of morning crossed the window's threshold. There would be, after all, another day for him. He was glad to be alone, yet afraid of what he would see when the other three beds in his room were unveiled. He listened to the sounds: a heavy, almost sullen exhalation of breath nearby, a timid snore from the corner opposite his own, and from the last bed, muffled by the green curtain, a soft, compelling groan emitted like a significant word.

But more terrible than what he might find in those other beds was his own wound. The bandages, when he looked toward the foot of the bed, tampered delicately with the edge of his vision.

His body seemed to be appallingly spread out, lost to him, the *he* that had been its everything. Had he imagined that he was the sole support of all of his cells? And that that *he* was really more significant than the cells of his lungs, his sweating fingertips? The democracy of the body was an awful thing to contemplate; he had believed he *was* what he thought; what he really was was an unstrung weight adrift.

The tube which led from his lung to a glass tank below the bed frightened him. He was afraid he would move involuntarily. The bed on its high-rising legs, with its immodest functionalism, its assertion of indifference, white, tubular, implacably virginal, was, he knew, given to sudden convulsions set off by levers at its foot. What if a nurse, ignorant of his wound, launched his bloody breast a foot in the air, or in some mania of mistaken efficiency, jack-knifed him?

The day was coming on strong now; it was the yellow, hot light of late August. Sleepers were waking. George heard a motor revving up beyond the window. There was an explosion of white as three nurses entered the room dancing; then they re-formed themselves into a starched militia.

It occurred to him suddenly that he had an appointment to meet Ernest in front of the bank. An exclamation of rage escaped his lips and, as muted as it was, turned the attention of the nurses toward him. They stared impassively. Then a voice just behind him said, "It speaks!"

He turned his head slowly. Another nurse stood there, a skinny little girl with a dead-white face, cheekbones like knuckles and a wide-lipped, smiling mouth. She had, he guessed, been there all along.

"I'm your nurse," she said.

"Can I move?" he whispered.

"Can you? Why don't you try?"

He brought his knees up slightly, then let them sink down at once. He was about to lift his left hand when he remembered the jar above his bed.

The nurse pointed up at it. "Breakfast, lunch and dinner for a while," she said.

204

"My God! What else am I plugged into?"

"Shush! Shame on you! You ought to sleep."

"Have you been here all the time?"

"Watching you . . ." she replied. Her smile looked friendly, yet it seemed to have some other dimension, to be a private smile, forbidding.

The curtains around the other beds were drawn. George felt the authoritative onset of pain, an end to partial anesthesia, and he wondered, knowing so little about the suffering of his flesh, how far *they* would let the pain continue. What if he cried out? What if he howled?

An elderly Negro curled up with his back to George groaned in a lonely, abandoned way. Across from him lay a man so thin only his kneecaps showed through the sheet. He was staring up at the top of the steel wheels in which his bed was suspended like a cam in a roller-skate wheel. To George's right, a young man reclined somewhat languorously, his elbow cocked to support a sharp chin. This last was observing George with a bland stare.

"Good morning," he said.

George said nothing. The nurse put her finger to her lips. George closed his eyes.

During the next few days he discovered it was as hard to hear the outside of things as it was to hear the inside. He hardly noticed faces; only procedures interested him. His pulse, his blood pressure, his respiration, the antibiotics, the sedatives, all grew intensely significant. He waited greedily for examinations and questions and hypodermics. Even the mysterious thoughtfulness of Miss Hyslop, his nurse, as she looked at the connections where the tubes entered his body, filled him with a kind of joy.

But what was said to him, what anything meant beyond

those words intended to probe and estimate, he didn't know. Miss Hyslop tired him, yet when she was gone for a few minutes, he longed for her return. Some inclination for conversation drove her to talk to him constantly. To her questions as to whether he had been to Puerto Rico, if he liked sports, what he taught, he countered with requests: The pillow was damp. . . . The sun was shining in his eyes. . . . When could he eat solid food? She began to look bewildered, as though she were stumbling around in her mind looking for a light switch. He wondered if he behaved so differently from other people.

The morning of his third day, the Negro patient disappeared. No one would say where he was. The young man with the sharp chin shook his head when George asked what had happened. The other man never spoke. George persisted until Miss Hyslop said, "He passed on," in such an angry whisper George understood that death was not to be mentioned here. People did not die in time but out of it. There was no way to speak about them.

That afternoon he was unplugged from the glucose and made to sit on the edge of his bed. They were trying to kill him. The floor rose up to smite him. Miss Hyslop held his arm and laughed.

"You old sissy!" she said.

"Shut up!" he said viciously.

Her lips trembled; her eyes rolled up.

"I'm sorry," he said. "I'm scared. Listen, I'm feeling much better."

"Hush," she said.

"How can you stand all of us?"

"Don't be sentimental," she said with unexpected severity. "Save your strength, Mr. Mecklin. Would you like a bedpan?"

"Not really," he said.

"You won't be needing me after tomorrow."

"Oh, God!" he said wretchedly.

"Now, Mr. Mecklin . . ."

"I feel awful."

She bent over him. "If you think you've got troubles, look around you."

"I don't want to look around me."

"You're all worked up. People always get emotional when their nurse leaves. You won't remember one thing about me within twenty-four hours." She looked at him rather wistfully then, but her mouth was set in a determined way, as though she had enunciated a truth basic to her sense of her self, a truth earned the hard way, without sentimentality.

He was going to weep. Miss Hyslop did something extraordinary. She ducked under his bed and started to thump the mattress. He began to laugh; he couldn't stop laughing. Her face appeared at the mattress level. The young man was leaning on his elbow as usual and grinning.

"All right, all right, Miss Hyslop," he said.

"I'm just getting you ready to see the police," she said, smiling now. "A detective is going to interview you."

"From under the bed?"

She laughed, fussing a little with her hair and her collar. He imagined her out of uniform, out of the hospital, walking down the street emitting faint sexual cries like the blips of a faulty radio. She was a little like Emma, he thought.

"Am I so much better really?"

"Pretty much," she said. "In another week or so, you'll be walking around."

The detective who arrived later that day kept his eyes scrupulously turned away from George's face. Perhaps he suspected that what he might see there would contradict the story George told him. Yes, George had known it was very late to visit people. But he'd been troubled—his wife had left him. He was desperate for company. Then when he'd gotten to the Devlins, he'd hesitated about walking in on them. Why had he left the car on the road? Well . . . he thought they might be asleep. "I wasn't in a reasonable state of mind," George said. The detective told him he was lucky. Yes. Everybody had been lucky, he said.

Miss Hyslop arrived with his antibiotic. After, when the detective had gone, Miss Hyslop, confirming his worst fears, stood at the foot of the bed and began to work the mechanism which raised the head of the bed.

"Let me be!" he pleaded with her, oblivious to the other patients, to everything except his terror at the thought that his chest would empty itself of his being, that his lungs would lie upon the sheets like dying fish. The world changed at an angle of thirty degrees. Miss Hyslop was smiling. "Good boy," she said.

She had told him he would be "all right." How could she tell him that? He was threatened from all quarters, by pneumonia, by the law, by his quelled and sluggish bowels, by the absolute knowledge that everything had changed for him and that his life could never be the same again.

Miss Hyslop dropped a letter on his lap.

It was from Emma. "How awful for you," she had written. "If you'd like me to come and see you, you can have someone phone me at Sarah Friedricks'. I called Lila a hundred times but she wasn't there. I also called Mr. Ballot in Westport. Where is the car? Fondly . . ."

"That bullet wasn't meant for me, Miss Hyslop," George said.

Miss Hyslop ran her fingers along his cheek. "You need a shave," she said.

She was gone the next morning and, just as she had said, he did forget about her. The Devlins helped. They arrived at noon, tiptoeing noisily to his bed.

"You don't look so hot," said Charlie.

"He looks marvelous, considering . . ." said Minnie.

Marvelous flew through the room, flapping its wet wings. Here were the marvelous-shouters who shut your mouth for you in an instant, who swallowed you up in a toad's gulp, standing by his bed.

"Marvelous . . ." she said coldly as she looked without expression at his bandages, his yellow tubes and glass jars.

"I'll get to the point," Charlie said. "I assume you're getting good care. . . . I just assume it. . . . I spoke to certain people. George, you admit it was pretty funny, your being there at the house at three in the morning. I mean, when no one's around except the worst ones. Let's say you were drunk. I'm not against that, emphatically not."

"Charlie, shut up!" said Minnie. "Charlie bends over backward to let people kick him around. I don't. Trevor saw his Daddy shoot a man. I'd rather a horse kicked you to death than for Trevor to have seen that." Her voice was low and steady; it exactly filled the space over George's head with no overlapping. "I don't know what you were up to," she went on. "What dirty thing you were up to. When your wife called me, I told her what a dirty man you were, looking through windows. Oh, yes . . . she's sorry. I told her not to bother with sorry. Not for you. That whatever it was, boys' behinds or looking in windows, I didn't care. Take your hand off me, Charlie. I said, I don't care.

But if you think you're going to sue us, or take us to court, or do anything at all, just try it. Try something." Incongruously, she smiled.

"Minnie's upset about the kid," Charlie said. "Now wait, Min. I mean, we'll pay for the private nurse, all the extras. You want a radio? But that's as far as we'll go. There was only a little mention of this in the news. Just a squib, you understand, about an accidental shooting. I can't afford . . . You know it was an accident. You admit that, don't you?"

"Get out!" said George. "Get out—or I'll scream!" He laughed, looking at Minnie; then he closed his eyes, feeling faint, knowing he could die in front of them, that it would not be remarkable to die, that he had lost his sense of exemption.

When he opened his eyes, the Devlins had gone and a nurse was there, holding his wrist, taking his pulse, that small thump beating up against nothing.

Gradually, perceptibly, the outer world reassembled itself within the reach of his thoughts. Ballot wrote and sent flowers. Martha Palladino called every day. But there was no further word from the Devlins and Emma. He was only mildly surprised at not hearing from Lila. Surely, Joe would have told her something. Yet he felt no special anger at her. It seemed to him now that all his relationships had been tenuous, sustained only by habit. Perhaps he was only more dutiful than Lila. He would have visited her. But did he really care any more about her than she cared about him?

Each day he went farther from his bed. The tank and the tubes had been removed. He was eating again. He was uncomfortable all the time, but he no longer had those appalling periods of pain when he lay stiff and silent, his eyes glued to the door, waiting for the nurse and the Demerol.

Sometimes he thought about Ernest—rather, visualized him, seeing his masked face in its commonness and mystery as he sprawled in a chair reading, or sitting at the kitchen table smoking Emma's cigarettes.

A few weeks after the night of the shooting, while George was walking cautiously down the corridor to see if there were any new magazines in the visitors' waiting room, the elevator doors opened just as he was passing them and Martha and Walling stepped out at the same moment. They had not known they were both coming to see George. He introduced them to each other and took them to the empty waiting room. Walling had shaved off his mustache; he looked older. He sat stiffly in a chair, looking gravely at George but with a suggestion of impatience. Martha's hands were trembling; she took a determined hold of her jacket. How strangely she was dressed! As though she wasn't sure what one wore in the world. Her face was heavily powdered with what looked like bath talc. There was something odd about her hair. A corkscrew curl or two lay like a fat cherub among the loose, straight strands. Even as he looked at her, George saw the curls gently unwind. She must have tried to put her hair up, he thought. She'd probably made faces at herself. Awkwardly she handed him two books. One was a paperback suspense story; the other was Edwin Muir's autobiography.

"Where did you get that?" he asked her, holding up the Muir. "It's hard to find."

"I've had it for years," she said. "I didn't know what

you'd like." Her voice was strained, and she sat very straight, as though to prevent it from fading away altogether. Walling reached into his pocket and brought out a puzzle, the kind in which by artful jiggling one tries to get little pellets into holes. He placed it on George's lap. "I didn't know what kind of toys you'd like," he said.

George's eyes filled with tears. Martha buttoned her jacket up to her neck. Walling sat, stricken. Dreams of nakedness . . . George couldn't stop. He wiped his cheeks with the back of his hands.

"When the private nurse left—I've forgotten her name —I did this. I'll stop in a minute. I'm sorry."

"You do have a strong response to gifts," Walling said.

"How are you?" asked Martha.

"All right," George said. The tears had stopped; his face felt cool and pleasant. "I think I can go home next week. I get tired quickly. But I'll be out of here, maybe Wednesday."

"Well . . . I thought you'd want to stay in the city for a while," Walling said. "I thought I could come and get you and drive you home. They took your car back. At least . . . until you know what you want to do. There's a faculty meeting on the fifteenth. It's a long distance for you to travel. There's room in the apartment. No, not that other place. I sublet that to a cabinetmaker. Maybe he'll buy a light bulb. The television finally broke down altogether. It had a fit—shot out lights like rockets. I thought I was going over the hill. Anyway, I can come up and pack a few things for you. Then you won't have to decide anything for a while."

George nodded. Between his present condition and decision, it was a long way.

212

"Minnie descended like a wolf on the fold," Martha said. "They're both terrified. She kept mentioning Charlie's influence with officials—all officials."

"They came to see me. . . ."

"She talks as if you'd tried to burn down the house."

"I suppose she said some pretty things about me."

Martha grinned. "Oh, yes. She did that." She reached in her pocket and took out a pair of brown leather gloves and began to smooth them. "I tried to reach your sister," she said.

The little room was very still. Walling touched his upper lip where the mustache had been. Martha was looking down at the old gloves.

"That was very good of you," said George.

"I couldn't reach her," Martha said. "I think maybe she's left the city." She held up the gloves. "Mummy's hands . . ."

"How did you know I was here?" George asked Walling.

"Ballot wrote me. He thought I might have seen you during the summer. . . . I don't know why. He suggested I see if you needed anything . . . cash, I suppose. Do you need anything?"

"Not a thing, except when you go to the house, there's a folder in the bedroom, somewhere, with checkbooks and insurance. If you'd bring that along, and the mail."

"What Ballot really wanted to know was whether you would be able to come back. He likes to keep things the way they are. He even backtracked on Rubin."

"Is Rubin staying?"

"No, not without tenure. And he couldn't get that."

A hospital silence fell; visitors and patient looked at each other across a gulf.

"The whole thing was my fault," George said suddenly.

Martha shook her head. "Don't say that," she said. "It doesn't matter now."

"Yes, it does."

Walling stood up. "I have to get back," he said. "There's a train in half an hour. I've got this thing about getting the train I've set my mind on."

"There are lots of trains," Martha said.

"That's the trouble," said Walling. "Once I miss the one I intend getting, it doesn't matter. See?"

Martha dropped her gloves in a wastebasket. "Imagine carrying those around all these years," she said. "George? Will you come to see me, after, when you're better?"

"Yes," he said.

Walling handed him a slip of paper. "That's my number. Have somebody call me when you're ready."

George stood up slowly, weak in the knees. He felt very tired.

"Good-bye . . . good-bye."

The days passed. In spirit, he had already left the hospital. He grew less interested in the ailments of other patients. At any rate, the character of his interest changed; it grew detached, lost its avidity. His bed, once neutral, then his refuge, was neutral once more. He lay on it lightly. He felt thinner, and was thinner. Shaving in the savage fluorescence of the bathroom, he observed his pale face. His nose appeared to have lengthened; his eyes stared deferentially into his mirror eyes.

No one paid much attention to him. A doctor told him he would be uncomfortable for some time, and even when he was completely healed, he would feel some pulling around the wound when the weather changed. Sometimes

George rested his hand lightly on the place where the bullet had entered, as though he were testifying to something.

Several members of the faculty sent him cards. Ballot wrote another note, saying that he had given George a light schedule to begin with, and what a dreadful experience it must have been, and oh, the modern world!

Then an envelope arrived with Martha's return address on it. Inside there was a clipping with two words written in smudged ink across the top: "I'm sorry." He didn't read it right away but held it by one corner as though it were on fire and burning and curling toward his fingers. Then he took hold of it with both hands.

LOCAL YOUTH IDENTIFIED

Peekskill—The body of a youth discovered August 25th behind the new Grand Union parking lot has been identified by Mr. Carl Jenkins, of 2113 3rd Street, as his son, Ernest, 18. Police said the youth belonged to a local gang of teen-agers. A member of the gang, Roy Kinsman, an unemployed garage mechanic, is being held for questioning. Jenkins had been beaten to death.

George walked to the bathroom, seeing Ernest's hands held out, the dried blood. He sat down on the toilet and rested his arms on the basin next to it. Then he put his head down. He had done nothing for him, nothing. Ernest, glimpsed through a train window at night, unknowable, cut off now forever.

The day before George was discharged from the hospital, a letter arrived from Lila.

"Dear George," she wrote. "I was shocked to hear of the accident (You can't imagine what it was like to find Joe's note beneath the door, so *absolutely* like him to write

215

instead of phoning—he can't bear to hear or speak of any-body's troubles) but relieved to know you are going to be all right. Emma finally called me and said you were well on your way. Also said you had separated. Poor George! I guess you have as many troubles as the rest of us."

Here, he put the letter down, smiled grimly, and went to the visitor's room where he sat for a while with a tattered copy of the *Saturday Evening Post* on his lap. The nurse came to get him; there were papers to sign and there was a detective to see him.

He went back to his room where he found the same detective whom he'd seen before. He grinned at George.

"Well. What do you say? You're up and around, hunh?"

"Fine," said George. "Aren't we all finished with this legal stuff?"

"Not all. See, we have to make sure, sure it was an accident, not a criminal incident."

They went over it again. With artful spontaneity, George confessed his drunken confusion that night, his distress, his lack of good sense. Yes, it was all true. He and Devlin had no scores to settle. He really didn't know the Devlins very well. In fact, he considered the whole thing his own responsibility. Seeing the bills spread out on his bedside table, he held them out to the detective. "You see? Devlin has paid them. Imagine having to take care of a man you shot in all righteousness!"

The detective looked at him suspiciously.

"I'm not a fool," he said.

"I am," replied George.

"Well—we'll see," he said and left. George finished Lila's letter.

"Now, I've got some surprising news. Claude and I are

going to stay in this town. It is very pretty, not quite sixty miles from Boston, and there's an artists' colony here, so the summers will probably be interesting. There's a nice old inn here with one of those English signs hanging in front of it, sort of the way I imagine an English 'pub' would look like. Of course, you'd know about that since you were actually in England. And, George, I'm the desk clerk. It hardly pays, but since I've told Philip I've moved out of the city, he's been sending the checks more regularly. *I do not understand this!*

"Even I finally got the idea about Joe, that it was a lost cause. But that *never* helps. Not when you're besotted like I was. It got so hideously clear. Oh, how it hurt! So I knew the only thing to do was to get far away. A friend told me about this place and at first I was just going to take a week's vacation and *think*. (That's why I've not been to visit you.) Well, we got here and I knew I couldn't go back to New York. Not for a long time. I could write pages about the farewells. But you don't want to hear about that now, I'm sure.

"We have this nice little house with a kitchen that looks out on a yard. It has two apple trees and they actually grow apples! The sunlight is shining through the windows right this minute and I have a cup of coffee next to my hand. Yesterday, Claude wouldn't get off the porch. He's just been hanging around me ever since we got here. But today, I just looked out the window, and Claude has almost reached the little fence behind the apple trees where there are two little kids playing. Maybe you're not as close to your childhood as I am, but I *know* what an effort it takes for him to walk out to those children. Can I do anything for you? That terrible man! As soon as I met him that night at their party, I knew he was bound to shoot someone, wasn't he?"

George tore the address off the envelope and threw the letter away. At ten the next morning, he was discharged from the hospital.

Walling had brought him clothes. As he dressed he was troubled, wondering where those other clothes had gone, the one's he'd been wearing that night. What had the hospital done with them? He couldn't really remember what he had been wearing. He said good-bye to the boy with the sharp chin who by now was swinging himself through the corridors on crutches. Then he walked over to Howard, who had seen George only when the bed swung up on its roller-skate wheel; hanging vertically for an instant, Howard's emaciated face, above the swaddling and the straps, had managed to intimate a smile. "Hello . . ." he would whisper to George across the room before the awful bed dropped him down so that his back, a vast bedsore, could be examined by a nurse. He would never get better. The only thing about Howard that moved were his eyes and the little finger of his right hand. George bent over and looked into the pale blue eyes. "Have a good time," Howard whispered.

The hospital was finished with him; he was nearly well, obsolete as far as they were concerned.

Through the glass doors he saw the day. As Walling pushed open the door, George passed from the incubator air of the hospital to the outdoors. It was September; the sky was clear, prismatic, blue. The air tasted like a freshly split watermelon. He saw his car in the parking lot.

"Your friend, Martha, helped me pack," Walling said as they got into the car.

"How was she?"

"We had a drink together—at nine o'clock this morning."

"Was she all right?"

Walling glanced at him. "A little nutty," he said. "But kindly. And how are you?"

"All right," George answered. "A little nutty."

He dozed as they drove down the Taconic to Hawthorne Circle, remotely aware of the car moving through the bright morning.

"How have things been with you?" he asked Walling later as they went through the tollgate at the Henry Hudson Bridge.

"I never know until the next day how I've been. Starting up with school gets me low."

"Don't you like any of it?"

"I guess I do, when I'm not anticipating it. I do hate those fall meetings. Some Negro educator is supposed to speak to us at the conference. He'll tell us what insular bastards we are."

"How do you know what he'll tell us?"

"Because we are."

Walling finally stopped in front of a new apartment house on Sixty-eighth Street. "You get out here," he said. "It'll take me a while to find a parking space at this time of day. Here's the key."

George opened the entrance doors, then decided to wait for Walling in the lobby. He sat on a vermilion plastic bench next to a plastic plant whose green tongues were coated with dust.

A number lit up above the elevator doors, and soon the elevator discharged two passengers, male and female, wearing sunglasses. The door closed behind them. George sat there feeling a profound interior silence, as though he'd been purged of all thought. Then Walling appeared at the door. George rose to let him in.

"The question is," Walling said, as the elevator rose, "which is more repulsive? This place or the one on Tenth Street? There must be some other way."

He took the key from George and bent to unlock his door, then pointed to a scrawl in red ink on the wall next to the doorbell.

"Betsy loves Paul," George read.

"Always the way of a lad with a lass," said Walling. "The bums."

George leaned forward. Lightly written in pencil after the two names were the words, "blimp" and "schmuck." George laughed. "Are those your additions?" he asked.

Walling looked. "Those are new since this morning," he said.

They walked into the apartment. Walling put down George's suitcase.

"This place is pure delicatessen," he said. "But my house is your house. Are you hungry?"

"Not yet."

"I hope you've noticed the delicacy with which I've avoided asking you how the hell you got shot, George. I mean—why a nice fellow like you was hanging around that house at that time of night?" He turned on a light, then said with a faintly embarrassed air, "If you want to tell me . . ."

George went from the foyer cubicle into the living room. There was nothing much to see: books, chairs, a lamp or two.

"All right," George said, "I'll tell you about it."

Walling sat down to listen.

Available in Norton Paperback Fiction

Andrea Barrett	*Ship Fever*
	The Voyage of the Narwhal
Rick Bass	*The Watch*
Simone de Beauvoir	*The Mandarins*
	She Came to Stay
Wendy Brenner	*Large Animals in Everyday Life*
Anthony Burgess	*A Clockwork Orange*
	Nothing Like the Sun
	The Wanting Seed
Frederick Busch	*Harry and Catherine*
Stephen Dobyns	*The Wrestler's Cruel Study*
Jack Driscoll	*Lucky Man, Lucky Woman*
Leslie Epstein	*King of the Jews*
	Ice Fire Water
Montserrat Fontes	*First Confession*
	Dreams of the Centaur
Leon Forrest	*Divine Days*
Paula Fox	*Desperate Characters*
	The Widow's Children
Carol De Chellis Hill	*Henry James' Midnight Song*
Linda Hogan	*Power*
Janette Turner Hospital	*Dislocations*
	Oyster
Siri Hustvedt	*The Blindfold*
Starling Lawrence	*Legacies*
Bernard MacLaverty	*Cal*
	Grace Notes
	Lamb
John Nichols	*The Sterile Cuckoo*
	The Wizard of Loneliness
Craig Nova	*The Universal Donor*
Jean Rhys	*Good Morning, Midnight*
	Leaving Mr. Mackenzie
	Quartet
	Wide Sargasso Sea

Josh Russell   *Yellow Jack*
Kerri Sakamoto   *The Electrical Field*
Joanna Scott   *Arrogance*
Josef Skvorecky   *Dvorak in Love*
Frank Soos   *Unified Field Theory*
Jean Christopher Spaugh   *Something Blue*
Rebecca Stowe   *The Shadow of Desire*
Kathleen Tyau   *A Little Too Much Is Enough*
Barry Unsworth   *After Hannibal*
                               Losing Nelson
                               Morality Play
                               Pascali's Island
                               Sacred Hunger
                               Sugar and Rum
David Foster Wallace   *Girl with Curious Hair*
Rafi Zabor   *The Bear Comes Home*